A Summer of Us

Chelsea Nyhan

Contents

CHAPTER 1

Every girl remembers her first kiss.

Mine was at the age of five. It was right after making numerous mud pies with my best friend Chase on a warm, sunny, August afternoon. It was quick, simple, and purely experimental. After the kiss, we giggled, wiped the "cooties" from our mouths, and ran over to the swing set.

Chase and I did everything together. We went swimming in his pond, played hide and seek, tried to catch fireflies, watched Pokémon, built snow men, picked dandelions, played catch - the list goes on and on. We share a special connection, one nobody else seemed to understand.

Chase was the son of my mother's best friend, Rebecca. For the first seven years of our lives, we were inseparable. Then, Chase's father got a job offer in California, causing the whole family to move 3,000 miles away.

Because we were only kids, we weren't able to use the phone line or email like our mothers. So instead, we wrote letters to each other. When I say letters, I mean a piece of notebook paper with a few messy sentences on it, enclosed in an envelope that our mothers filled out with the mailing information. We kept the letters going for a few months. Gradually over time, the letters became less frequent. Eventually, they stopped. Although our mothers continued to stay in touch, Chase and I moved on with our lives. We grew up, made new friends and forgot about each other.

Until last week, when my mother brought up his name for the first time in a number of years.

"Hayden, do you remember Rebecca and her son, Chase?" His name felt so unfamiliar, and sounded so foreign. Yet, it struck some melancholy into my heart. It was as if my brain didn't remember, but my heart did.

"Vaguely," I muttered.

"Well, I was talking to Rebecca on the phone the other night and she invited us to spend the summer at their house."

"In ... California?" Slowly, it was all coming back to me.

"Yes. They've got a beautiful house in Santa Monica, right on the shore," my mother said, with a cheerful tone. She wasn't very good at hiding her excitement.

"And Rebecca wants us to come?"

"Yes. She thinks it would be a great way to reconnect and get our families close again." A bright, pearly grin appeared on my mother's face. "Your father thinks it's a great idea too! He said he misses John's knee-slapping jokes."

I couldn't tell if I wanted to go or not. So mentally, I made a pro and con list.

Pro: Going to California and getting out of boring Connecticut for a while.

Con: Spending my summer going into senior year away from my friends.

Pro: Seeing my childhood best friend after spending ten years apart.

Con: Having it be completely awkward and starting fresh because we've changed and no longer know each other well.

Pro: Making my mother happy.

Con: Possibly making myself unhappy.

My mother must have interpreted my internal thinking as displeased silence, because she said, "If you don't want to, Honey, I'll understand. But, if you don't go, your father and I can't go because as parents we can't leave you home alone for three months. I know it's very last minute, and I shouldn't have sprung this on you. I was just so excited to finally see my best friend, but it's okay if you say no."

Oh crap, I thought. I hate when parents pull the guilt trip.

I squeezed my eyes shut, took a deep breath, and said, "Fine, I'll go."

The expression on my mother's face was priceless - a combination of joy, relief, thankfulness and excitement. It was a bittersweet feeling to see my mother so happy about a sacrifice I had made. Despite being far away from my friends in, an unknown area, with someone I hardly knew anymore, I strongly believed that Karma would help me out in the end.

Chapter 2

Despite my efforts to suppress all my worries about California, they somehow managed to rise above the surface on the 9-hour flight. Sitting in my restricted airplane seat, looking out the small plastic window, I couldn't help but let my mind wander:

What's California like? How's the beach? What will the girls be like? Will I make friends? What's it going to be like seeing Chase again? Has he changed? Does he look different? Will we get along? Has he forgotten the past?

One question led to another and it was hard to stop. The questions consumed me, driving me to a point of insanity. I needed my brain to stop, so I tried reading a book - The Adventures of Huckleberry Finn. However, my attempt to distract my brain was unsuccessful. Huck Finn reminded me too much of Chase. From what I could remember, Chase was always an adventurous and incredibly smart kid, like Huckleberry.

Frustrated with myself, I snapped my book closed. Eventually, I gave up and decided to take a snooze, hoping my brain would shut off and my subconscious would slip into a world without worries.

I was right. My mother woke me up from my peaceful serenity, and told me we were landing soon. Luckily, my mind was too groggy from the nap to ask pestering questions.

After loading off the plane and collecting our checked baggage, we reached the airport exit where we were supposed to meet up with Rebecca, John, and Chase. Looking around the area for them brought the nerves back. My stomach churned, my hands grew clammy, my leg began to bounce in anxiousness. I was moments away from him.

"There they are!" My mother exclaimed with a shrill of her voice. I looked in the direction she was pointing too. Rebecca was still as gorgeous as I remembered, with her tall, skinny physique, straight blonde hair, and pearly white smile. Unlike Rebecca, John looked as though the ten years did age him. He was sporting new thick-rimed glasses and salt & pepper hair. Not to mention, he looked frail and weak, as if he lost 20 pounds.

Then, I noticed Chase. The moment my eyes looked upon him, I felt my heart sink low into my stomach. He looked the same, just older, taller, and buffer. Chase still had that shaggy blond hair that got lighter in the summer, and those crystal blue eyes.

He looked the same, but did he act the same?

My mother and Rebecca rushed towards each other, leaving Chase, John, Dad, and I to lag behind.

"Stacy!" Rebecca's melodic voice said. She threw her arms around my mother. "I've missed you so much!"

By the time their embrace ended, all of us had catch up to them.

Rebecca stepped towards me and put her hands gently on my face. "You look so grown up, so mature, Hayden. Look at your hair, it's such a beautiful chocolate color. You're absolutely stunning."

I blushed slightly. Rebecca always had a way of making me feel like the most beautiful girl in the world, even when I knew I wasn't. As she hugged me, the classic Rebecca scent - Chanel No.5 with a hint of Downy Laundry Detergent - filled my nostrils. Closing my eyes, I let her scent take me back to the old days.

John, who had already greeted my father with a wisecrack, was next to greet me. Quickly, I looked over at Chase, who was catching up with my mother.

"Hey kiddo," John said, giving me a quick body squeeze.

"Hi Uncle John."

"God, I love that you still call me that," he said, with a large grin.

"Only if you'll still call me kiddo!"

"You've got yourself a deal," he said. He held out his hand, and I shook it. I felt him slip something through our palms. When we released, I saw he had given me a $50 bill. My eyes widened at him. "Shhh, it's our little secret. Spend it wisely, young grasshopper."

John was probably the greatest man I had ever met. He was always funny, kind and incredibly giving. He knew when to act like a father, and when to act like a kid.

After John went to greet my mother, I knew it was time - the moment I had waited for. Our eyes met, and we slowly walked towards each other.

"Hey," said Chase, softly.

"Hey."

Chase wrapped his arms around me and I wrapped mine around his neck. I felt his buff pecs against my chest. Feeling safe in his arms, I let my eyes slowly close. This hug felt so similar yet so different than the ones we used to give to each other. It had the same effect - warm, safe, comforting. But it was more tender and passionate than the ones we use to have as kids. Despite whether or not I was reading too much into this, it felt good to be reconnected with chase, after being apart for so long.

Chapter 3

Our hug ended just as Rebecca suggested we head to the cars, which left us no time to catch up. Chase offered to carry my luggage and we exchanged glances while walking to the parking lot.

When we reached the parking lot, I noticed they had two cars with them - probably because we were one too many for a 5-person car.

"So why don't the adults go in John's car, and the two teenagers go in Chase's car," Rebecca said.

This is when I started to panic. Being alone, in the car with Chase? What if it was completely awkward? Afraid that my legs would give out from the nerves, I quickly jumped into the passenger seat.

Chase loaded my luggage into the backseat of his Jeep Wrangler before hopping in the driver's seat.

"You look good, Hayden," Chase said. He reached out, and twisted a lock of my hair between his fingers. "I like your hair long and wavy."

"Thanks," I said, nervously. I grew out my hair when I was nine, so this was the first time Rebecca and Chase had seen my "new" hair. Chase let go of my hair, and started the car engine.

Once we were on the road, I asked him, "What's the one thing you miss about Connecticut?"

"Oh, that's a tough one. I'd have to say . . . snow and you."

Good answer. "Really?"

"I mean, yeah! It never snows here. No more snowmen, or snow angels, or snowball fights, or sledding! And it really sucked leaving you. I'm really glad you came," Chase said, resting his hand on my bare thigh.

"Yeah, me too." I put my hand on top of his. Why did I feel so weird about this? Like what he was saying was almost too good? "I have a question."

"Shoot."

"Why did we stop writing to each other?"

"I wish I knew. I mean, I guess just after a while, the distance caused us to drift apart and we just moved on. But, hey look at us now! Reunited at last and it feeeels so good!" He belted, very off key.

I couldn't help but laugh. "Please, never sing again!"

"What?" He laughed. "You don't like my singing? I was totally thinking about trying out for American Idol. Don't you think I could win?"

"Oh definitely! Good luck with that," I teased.

"You're sarcasm is not appreciated." He gave my hand a playful squeeze.

We spent a few minutes in silence, which gave me a chance to look at the landscape. It was beautiful - clear blue sky, tons of palm trees, and a stunning coastline. This was paradise.

After the scenic drive, we pulled up to Levine's beach house. Rebecca and John were already given my parents a tour of the house.

Chase got my bags and showed me around. Just like the area, their house was beautiful and tropical. Colors of blue, yellow, and green were accented throughout the house. Large windows showed a perfect view of the crashing ocean, and the scent of salt and fresh air filled each room.

My room was two doors down from Chase's. My room had a white whicker dresser, a queen sized bed with a powder blue comforter, French doors that lead onto a terrace, paintings and frame photographs of the Pacific coastline, and an old rocking chair. It was simple, soothing, and serene.

I was in the middle of unpacking when Chase knocked on my door. "Hayden, I'm going down to the beach. You want to come?"

How could I turn down such an offer? "Yeah, lemme just get changed."

I quickly pulled out a blue string bikini, a white cotton button-down, jean shorts, flip flops, and my black ray-ban wayfarers. I got dressed, keeping the white button down open so that it exposed my bikini.

Chase was waiting in the living room. He was only wearing his swim trunks, revealing his toned upper body.

"Let's go!"

Chase and I walked outside, down the hill, then onto the beach. It was lively and busy, but not overcrowded.

There were beach volleyball players, surfers, lifeguards, children, senior citizens, young adults, middle aged parents, teenagers, college kids partying, and so on and so on.

We passed by two young kids building a sandcastle - one boy, one girl. The girl threw sand in the boy's face, and they started a sand fight. Chase saw them too, and looked over at me. We both laughed, knowing that used to be us.

Chase was about to show me the populated pier, when we both heard a girl scream, "CHASE!"

Stopping in our tracks, we turned around to see where the noise had come from.

A petite, blonde, bubbily girl dressed in pink, came rushing over to us. "Chase, baby! There you are! I've been like calling your name for like ten minutes!"

She smothered him with a big, sloppy kiss. Chase appeared to be caught off-guard, and shot me a panicked glance. I wasn't sure what exactly was going on, but I did not like it.

CHAPTER 4

Who could blame the guy? He had a girlfriend, big deal. I wasn't angered or saddened by this; I was just rather annoyed by the fact that he was a total flirt in the car. Truth was, we were best friends. Back in the day, we kissed, we loved each other, but as friends and nothing more.

"So I'm going to go walk around," I said. Seeing that girl hang all over Chase made me want to gag. "I'll see you back at the house."

I was walking away, trying to figure out where to go. I felt Chase tug on my shoulder and spin me around.

"It's not what it looks like," he huffed.

"Look Chase, you don't have to feel sympathetic. You have a girlfriend! I wouldn't be surprised if you didn't," I said.

"Jessie isn't my girlfriend. Well, she was, but I broke up with her last May! We're just friends!"

It looks like she's got a lot more than friends on the brain, I wanted to say. But I didn't. Instead I said:

"It's okay. Go hang out with her; she'll obviously have an aneurism if you don't. I'll be fine," I said, before turning around and proceeding to talk again.

"Wait," he said, tugging me again, "let me make it up to you. 5 o'clock, meet me back at the house. I have a little surprise for you."

"Okay," I said. We exchanged smiles before heading in separate directions.

I had no idea where to go, so I stuck close to the beach. After aimlessly walking back and forth on the beach, I decided to park myself in a vacant spot, close to the shore.

For a while, I sat in the sand and watched the crowd of people swim. I watched as the kids ran in and out, only wadding out a few inches. I watched as the surfers hitched a wave, rode it for a while, and then wiped out. I watched as the mature couple treaded water for what seemed forever in deep water, far from the crowded beach.

Just sitting and watching, I couldn't help but get lost in my thoughts. Mostly, I thought about the past. Not particularly my past, but the past in general. If you think about it, the past is a strange yet amazing thing. A person's past shapes who they are now. Without our past, without our own personal history, we would be nothing.

But, how easy it was to forget the past. Sometimes, it's hard to remember the experiences and feelings we used to have.

Sometimes, our pasts are so distant that they get replaced by our presents.

And that's what worried me the most about Chase. Not his ex-girlfriend, not spending the summer in California with him, but our past. Could he have forgotten everything we shared together? Could our past mean nothing to him anymore?

Before I knew it, it was time to go back and meet up with Chase. And I was a lot more nervous than I should have been.

Chase was already waiting for me on the front porch. Dressed in cargo shorts, boat shoes, and an American Apparel sweatshirt.

"Ready?" He asked.

"Yeah," I said. "Uh should I change into something else?"

He took a minute to check me out. "No, you look perfect!"

Eagerly, Chase grabbed my hand, pulled me back to the beach, and led me onto a sandy path.

"So, what do you think of all of this?" he asked, after several minutes of walking. "I mean, what do you think of seeing each other for the first time in like a decade?"

This question caught me off guard. It wasn't a surprising matter, I was just shocked to hear it coming from him.

"Um . . . it's interesting. I mean, strange, but in a good way."

"Can I be really cliché and sappy for a minute, and say that this feels like finding that one puzzle piece that I lost a long time ago, and now I feel sort of complete?"

How cute, yet incredibly cheesy. And despite the fact that I really wanted to say awwww, I stopped myself, gave him a playful shove and said, "Leave the romance for Shakespeare."

He laughed at himself and said, "How did I know you were going to say something like that? I'm glad you haven't changed a bit, Ace."

Ace. That was the nickname he gave me after I told him I wanted to be a journalist when I was six.

"I can't believe you still remember that," I said, hopping over a piece of driftwood.

"Of course I do," he said. Casually, he took my hand and intertwined his fingers with mine. "So do you still want to be a big time journalist, reporting the news, traveling around the world, finding the scoop on the latest story?"

"I don't think so. I'm leaning towards going into the business field."

Chase stopped dead in his tracks. "You can't be serious."

"What?"

"I just can't see you as a business woman. You're just too energetic and interesting to be stuck behind a desk doing all that calculating and formulating."

Maybe Chase had a point. Or maybe, he was trying to give out a compliment.

"Well, what about you! What do you want to do?"

"When I cross that road, I'll take it. But, honestly, I don't need to make a lot of money or become some worldwide house name. If I can just stay close to the beach, then I'll be fine," he said, kicking some sand up in the air. "The beach is a place where no worries exist. Just the smell of saltwater in the air, the sound of crashing waves, the sight of blue monsters swirling in a pattern - I don't need a big house or a fancy car, as long as I have the beach."

I was pretty blown away by this. How passionate and deep Chase was about this place. But it was in no way surprising. He was always the kind of person who loved to be outside, staying active, enjoying the pleasures of nature.

"Wow Chase," I said. "That was really deep."

He put his arm around my waist. "Now, don't go feeding my ego."

Chapter 5

We spent the remainder of the walk laughing, chatting, and catching up. Chase talked about his boarding school, and how his dad hasn't been feeling well. I talked about my high school, and how my parents don't sleep in the same bed anymore. He talked about his job as a lifeguard, and I talked about my job as a guitar teacher. He talked about how a lot of his friends have been getting in trouble; I talked about how a lot of my friends were turning into whores.

One of the greatest things about our friendship was our communication. We told each other everything, just as we used to. Of course, the topics were more complex and mature now, but it was nice to know we still had that connection. Unlike every other guy I knew, I felt comfortable and secure with Chase.

"Oh, we're almost there! Close your eyes," Chase said. "I want this to be a little bit of a surprise."

"If I can't see, there's a good chance I will walk into something and seriously injure myself." It took me a few years to finally accept the fact that I was a Grade-A klutz.

"Don't worry, I'll lead you," Chase said. I closed my eyes, and felt Chase wrap his arm around me to lead the way. "No peeking."

As any normal kids would, Chase and I played Hide and Seek on a daily basis. However, after numerous occasions, Chase had to become the permanent seeker because I had the habit of opening my eyes and peeking.

As if I was a puppet, Chase moved my body and directed me safely to our destination. I was almost sad when it was over, because I loved feeling his body pressed up against mine.

Was it wrong of me to be so attracted and interested in my best friend? No matter how hard I tried to suppress my feelings, they just kept rising to the surface. I knew I didn't want to screw up what we had, so I had to constantly remind myself that we were just friends . . .

"Ready? One, two, three - open."

There we stood, at the entrance of the famous Santa Monica Pier - home to restaurants, bars, shops, an aquarium, and a Ferris wheel.

"Chase, this is amazing!"

"I'm glad you like it, Ace. Come on, we've got a lot to do," he said, taking my hand.

We glided along the pier, listening to the music that drifted out of restaurants, and glancing in stores to see if they had anything interesting.

"So, what should we do first? Ferris wheel or dinner?" Chase asked.

"Oh, tough decision. I'm going to say . . . Ferris wheel."

Since it was still a little light out still, the Ferris wheel line wasn't too bad, so Chase and I jumped in line. It was actually perfect timing, because we got to see the sun beginning to set over the ocean, painting the sky with colors of purple, orange, pink, and red.

"Do you remember that year when we went to the Memorial Day Fair together, and you got sick on the Ferris wheel? I swear, you could see hints of cotton candy in the vomit," Chase said, laughing at the memory.

"Hey! At least I wasn't the one who puked up all his Twiz-zlers on the drive home from Hersey Park," I rebutted. Two could play at that game.

Chase's cheeks blushed with embarrassment. "To this day, I still get really car sick."

"It takes a real man to admit his weaknesses," I joked.

"I gotta be a big, strong real man for my lady," he joked back, flashing his arm muscles.

If only it wasn't a joke, if only I was his lady . . .

"What's wrong?" Chase asked, snapping me out of my wish list. "You're not feeling sick from the ride, are you?"

"What? Oh no, I'm fine."

"Good," he said with relief. "Hey, maybe it's a good thing we didn't eat first. I'd rather you not puke up the delicious dinner I bought you."

"It was one time!" I said, exasperated.

"Okay," Chase said, with a devious smile.

After the ride ended, we decided to grab dinner. Chase led us to a restaurant called the Sandy Shell. The place was so packed, that the waiting line was out the door.

"Uhh, Chase? Did you make a reservation?"

"Nah," he said, before forcefully pushing past the people in line.

"Maybe we should go somewhere else," I called, trying to keep up with him. He didn't respond, so I assumed he didn't hear me. After saying "excuse me" and "sorry" about a billion times, I caught up to Chase who was at the hostess' desk.

"Right this way, Mr. Levine," she said, slipping two menus into her hand.

Lagging behind her, I asked, "How did you get us seated without a reservation? Judging from the size of that line, it must be like a forty minute wait."

"Let's just say, I'm pretty tight with the boss."

The hostess sat us at an outside table, with a view of the ocean, extending all the way down the Pacific Coastline. By now, the sun always almost gone, leaving a smoky effect with vague hints of remaining orange. The only word that could describe it was perfection.

CHAPTER 6

After we spent a couple minutes admiring the view, then ordering our food, and talking a little, I excused myself to go to the bathroom.

While washing my hands, I noticed the girl standing next to me, who was the last person I wanted to see...

"Oh, I know you," she said, when she saw my death glare. "You're that chick that's staying with Chasie. We sort of met, but I'm Jess."

"Hi," I said coldly. Maybe I had nothing personally against her, but the fact that she was Chase's creepy, in denial ex-girlfriend was enough reason to not be her #1 fan. "I'm Hayden."

"So what are you doing here?" She asked with curiosity.

"Uh ..." I decided I should just tell her the truth, but make it seem as casual as possible. "I'm out with Chase, he's just showing me around.

"Fun," she said, with a fake tone. "Isn't Chasie like the best?"

A trick, of course. Something I was too smart to fall for. "Yeah he's okay."

"Yeah?" Her face instantly hardened. "Well, make sure it stays that way, or else I swear I will destroy your life."

When a person threatens and thinks they can mess with me, it pushes me over the edge. "Oh no, I'm so scared of the short, blonde pipsqueak," I said sarcastically.

"Bitch, know your place. You're an outsider, a foreigner. This is my territory, not yours. Chase is mine, not yours, and don't you forget that. Mess with me, and I'll mess with you."

My mouth dropped, and she exited the bathroom before I could respond. You know those iconic, blonde, popular bitches in high school movies that think they're better than everyone and ruin the lead characters life? That was Jessica. She was my own personal Regina George.

Soaking in the shock, I didn't even realize someone else was in the bathroom until I heard the toilet flush.

A beautiful, sultry, edgy girl dressed in a waitress outfit came out of the bathroom stall.

"Don't let her get to you. She's not even worth a thought."

I was relieved to find out that not all the girls in California were as stuck up and rude as Jessica was. "Thank you."

"No problem. And don't listen to what she says, do what you want, she's not the boss of you," the girl said, rinsing her hands.

"Very true, thanks! I'm Hayden."

"Carmen," she said. "From what I gathered, you're not from around here. Do you know anyone else other than Chase and the bitch from hell?"

"Nope," I said, which made me feel rather pathetic. I felt incredibly friendless here.

"Oh, I see. Well, I'd love to show you around and introduce you to some chill people," Carmen said.

"Thanks, I'd love that!"

"Alright! Give me your arm?" I extended my arm in front of her, and she pulled out a pen from her waitress pouch. She wrote down her number across my forearm and told me to call her tomorrow if I was looking for something fun to do. Then, we both left the bathroom and went in separate directions.

Chapter 7

As I walked back to the table, I was debating if I should tell Chase about the little run-in I had with Jessica. I knew he would probably want to know, but I also knew that it would only cause more unnecessary drama. I decided against telling him.

"Ready to go?" Chase asked.

"Sure," I said.

We paid the check, left the restaurant, and resumed our pier stroll. The pier was quieter because the sun had set, and bars were just beginning to open. The bad thing about being 17 was we were too old to go home and too young to go out clubbing and drinking.

"What would you like to do?" Chase asked, after aimlessly walking.

"I don't know, you tell me. What is there to do here at this time?"

"Hmm . . ." He pondered. I watched his face as his eyebrows crinkled together in concentration. Suddenly, they rose. "I've got it! Come with me!"

Chase broke into a full on sprint. Accepting the challenge, I raced after him, trying to eliminate the distance between us. Quickly, I caught up to him. We ran side by side, down the pier, through the sandy path, to the deserted beach.

"Take . . . your . . . clothes . . . off," Chase panted, clearly out of breath.

"What?" I huffed. Overwhelmed with heat and shortage of breath, I thought my ears were playing a joke on me. I watched as Chase removed his shirt, showing me those solid abs again.

"Yeah," he said, regaining his normal breathing pattern. "We're going skinny-dipping."

"You can go skinny-dipping, I'll wear my bathing suit," I said, unbuttoning my shirt. I was so thankful that I didn't get changed for the date.

He made a pouty face. "Please? It's no fun if you wear your bathing suit! That defeats the liberating, exciting, thrilling purpose of skinny-dipping."

Chase made a good point. But the last time he had seen me naked was when we used to take baths together when we were like two.

"Okay, fine. But one condition: you have to walk ahead of me."

Chase pursed his lips together and said, "Deal."

Chase took a few steps forward, his back facing me. I watched as his shorts dropped, then his boxers. I slipped off my bikini, feeling incredibly self conscious and exposed. I walked behind him, lagging only a few paces.

He gracefully dove into the crashing water, which looked bone-freezing cold. Knowing Chase would rise to the surface any minute, I bit down on my lip, squeezed my eyes closed and lunged towards the water.

At first, a bitter chill ran through my body - but in a few seconds, the chill turned into numbness. I let the water gently cascade over me and rock my body, until my lungs had no air left.

"Nice isn't it?" Chase said, once I reached the surface.

"Yeah," I whispered. Floating on my back, I closed my eyes and let the water control the movement of my body.

"You forgot you're naked, didn't you?" Chase chuckled. My eyes shot open and saw Chase checking my body out. His eyes were sparkling with desire and his lips were in the form of a devious grin.

"HEY! You perv!" I splashed him. He splashed me back. We broke into an epic water fight, like the ones we used to have in his pond.

"Okay, okay," Chase laughed, shielding his face. "I hate to end this skinny-dipping party, but we should probably head back soon."

Chase was swimming back to the shore when I yelled, "LAAAAME."

Before I could react, Chase was already swimming towards me, full speed.

"I'll show you lame!" He yelled, before grabbing onto my shoulders and dunking my head under the water. With all my force, I tried to push against his hard grip, but he was ten times stronger than I was. Suddenly, I realized that I was pressed up against his naked body, which made me immediately stop my attempt to escape. I'm not exactly prude (even though I'm still a virgin) but being so close to Chase intimidated me for some reason. Probably because right now, I was unsure about how I felt. I was trapped in this grey area with him, which terrified me.

Chapter 8

A few seconds after I stopped struggling, Chase pulled me up. "SHIT Hayden! You scared me! I thought you passed out from loss of oxygen or something!!"

"Whoops!" I said innocently, adding a shrug and a wink.

"Shall we go?" Chase said. I nodded and we swam back to the beach. Chase walked in front of me, giving me a view of his bare butt. I got out, and pulled on my clothes. Shivering, I realized the water was much warmer than the air.

"Here," Chase said, slipping off his American Apparel sweatshirt. He draped it over my shoulders and wrapped his arm around me. He rubbed his hand, up and down my body, trying to create friction and warmth.

When we were inside of the house, I ran over to the couch and pulled a thick blanket over myself. Chase flopped down next to me, and tugged the blanket so it covered him as well.

"Shall we watch a movie?" I nodded eagerly. He scrolled through the movie listings. "Any requests?"

"Surprise me," I said.

Chase ended up choose Risky Business, with Tom Cruise - a film that satisfied both of us.

"You know, I had a really great time tonight," I said, during the opening credits.

"Me too, Hayden." Chase and I gazed at each other, holding eye contact for several moments. Then, with an exchange of sly smiles, we both turned our attention back to the film.

I rested my head on Chase's cozy, warm lap, and before I knew it, I fell asleep.

When I woke, Chase was gone. Another blanket had been wrapped over me, and a pillow was under my head to replace Chase's lap.

I saw a note tapped to the coffee table: Lifeguarding. Come find me - Chase.

I got dressed in a black bikini, oversized t-shirt, and my ray-bans. Quickly, I made my hair and face look somewhat acceptable before heading down to the beach.

After a few walks up and down the beach, I found him sitting in a lifeguard chair next to another guy. As I walked towards him, I noticed the hot aviators he was wearing (such a turn on).

I cranked my neck to look at Chase. He looked mighty and powerful, sitting up there, the sun glaring over the top of his head. When he saw me, he gracefully jumped down from the lifeguard chair.

"Hey Ace," Chase said. The other lifeguard jumped down as well. "I want you to meet my best bud, Tyler."

"Nice to meet you," Tyler said. "I've heard loads about you."

I really wanted to ask what he's heard about me, but I resisted the urge. "Nice to meet you too!"

Tyler was really, really attractive. He had short, jet-black hair, and an olive complexion and dark, chocolate eyes - the complete opposite of Chase. Although Tyler seemed nice, I couldn't help but get a cocky, player vibe from him.

"Chase told me you really liked my family's restaurant," Tyler said, with an unhidden grin.

"Oh, so you're Chase's secret connection to the Sandy Shell," I said, peeking a glance at Chase.

"Guilty," Chase admitted. Tyler saluted me before climbing back onto the lifeguard chair. "So anyway, I get off at six, so why don't we meet up at the house around then, and I'll take you out for a boat ride?"

"Okay, sounds fun," I said, trying to hide my excitement. "See you later!"

Since I had seven hours to waste, I was able to accomplish much. First, I tanned for about 2 hours. Then, I headed back to the house. I unpacked, showered, and then tried to pick out my outfit for the boat ride.

Should I go casual? Should I go dressy? Why was I over thinking this?

I settled on a lavender beaded tank, black shorts, gladiator sandals, and my black bikini - it was casual with a touch of flirt. I French braided my hair and wore minimal make up.

By the time I was ready, I still had a solid 30 minutes. So, I decided to sit on the back porch and strum on my acoustic guitar.

C/G, F/G, E minor, D minor, F major, C major, A minor

The things I think I did

I do, I think I did

But the things I think I did

When I was a kid

I couldn't understand a word that they were saying

But still I hung around and took it all in

I wouldn't join in the games that they were playing

It went by, it went by, in a flash

I heard clapping behind me when I finished the song.

"Not bad, not bad. But my singing is better," Chase said, coming around to face me. "Ready to go, rockstar?"

CHAPTER 9

We walked along that sandy path again, but in the opposite direction. Eventually, we reached a private dock, with three boats tied up. One yacht, a skimmer, and a medium sized motorboat.

"Which one?" I asked. Chase pointed to the motorboat, which was the perfect choice - not too big, not too small, just right in the middle, like Goldie Locks.

Chase hopped on first, then played gentleman, and offered his hand to help me onto the boat.

"Shawty call bow seat!" I exclaimed, racing for the front of the boat. Flopping onto the leathery cushioned seat, I got the best view.

With a roar of the engine, we were off. Like the night before, It was a perfect sight. From my perspective, it looked like we were driving right into the sunset. Closing my eyes, I let the wind whip against my face.

"CAPTAIN JACK SPARROW GOT NOTHING ON ME!" Chase exclaimed, accelerating even more. Chase made sharp turns, speeding across, creating huge waves. Eventually, he stopped and put the boat in neutral.

Chase walked to the front, and plopped down next to me. He casually slipped his arm around my shoulders. He turned to face me, his blue eyes piercing into mine.

"So …" he said.

"So …" I whispered back.

"I still can't believe you're here, after 10 years of being apart. You haven't changed a bit. I've really missed you, Ace."

I bit down on my bottom lip and said, "I've missed you too."

"Do you remember our first kiss?"

"Slightly," I said, softly.

"Maybe this will jog your memory."

Chase grabbed a lock of my hair and pushed it behind my ear. He tilted my chin, and pulled his face up to mine - our lips only a centimeter away from touching.

3…

2 . .

1.

Touchdown.

His sweet, warm breath mixed with mine. I wrapped my arms around his neck, and he pulled my body closer to his.

Had I been expecting this? Did I want this? Was this going to ruin our friendship? Did he want a relationship?

Questions squirmed inside my head, but I forced them away. Right now, I would enjoy this, and deal with the questions and consequences later.

He drew a line of kisses - from my mouth, to my check, to my neck, up to my ear.

Leaning back on the seat, I let Chase lay on top of me. We stopped kissing, and I looked up at him. His crystal blue eyes were bright with passion and affection. He kissed me again, soft and tenderly.

I'm not sure how long we were making out for, but by the time we finished, it was pitch black.

Knowing that we should probably go back, Chase revved up the boat engine.

"Ace, you want to drive?" He asked. Eagerly, I jumped up and grabbed the steering wheel. "Okay, easy girl. Now, put your hand on the gas drive." He grabbed my hand and placed it on the knob. "You adjust it when you want to change gears or speed. And, then you've got the steering wheel, and you're good to go."

When I pushed the knobbing gas-thingy, the boat zoomed across the water. I kept it at that speed, and drove the steering wheel, directing the boat through the red and green buoys.

Driving the boat made me free, liberated, empowered.

Before I knew it, we were at the dock. Chase leaped out, reeled the boat in closer, and tied it up.

Once again, we walked along that sandy path, holding hands, chattering about nonsense.

"I had a lot of fun today, Hayden," Chase said, once we reached the house.

"Yeah, me too," I said, before yawning.

Chase walked me to my bedroom door. "So, look, there's a party tomorrow night. You should go with me."

"Okay," I said.

"You're tired," he concluded. "I can tell. Goodnight, Hayden." He gave my lips a soft peck.

"Night, Chase," I said, before opening my door.

A combination of loud voices woke me up the next morning. I assumed it was just all of the parents, but I decided to get up and investigate.

I was . . . so wrong.

There, in the kitchen stood Chase, with Jessica and Tyler. Tyler was counting out money.

"You win bro, fair and square," Tyler said, handing the cash over. "I can't believe you actually got her to kiss you so quickly."

My mouth dropped open. Were they talking about me?

"Looks like we have a visitor," Jessica giggled. "Whoops, you weren't supposed to know about this! Sorry, mahhhh bad."

Tears flooded to my eyes, my throat closed up and developed a lump, the room was spinning. I starting walking towards the back door, that led outside. That walk turned into a brisk, power walk. And from there, it turned into a run.

"Hayden! Wait!" I heard Chase call out after me, but I didn't wait, I didn't stop.

Chapter 10

I wandered around the beach aimlessly, until I found a deserted area. Collapsing onto the sand, I curled up into a ball and cried. How could he do this to me? Did he really not care about me?

And yet, despite his actions, I could only blame myself. I should have been smarter, stronger, and more cautious. I shouldn't have trusted him so quickly, trusted that he was the same guy from 10 years ago. Reality was, time changes people, and I should have accepted that instead of denying it.

When my eyes could no longer produce tears, I sat up. Feeling the cold wind, I pulled my knees to my chest, and stared at the vast, over-fogged ocean.

Right now, I felt as though I was stranded in the middle of the freezing Pacific Ocean. Clumps of seaweed wrapped around my ankle, trying to pull me under. But, I had to fight it, I had to be strong, I had to keep my head above water and swim back to the shore.

Composing myself, I got up, brushed the sand from my clothes, and staggered back to the house. I felt dead inside, like a walking zombie, but I pushed on.

Chase was sitting on the section of the beach that was right in front of the house.

"For god sake, Hayden! I searched everywhere for you! I swear, it's not what you think!"

"Oh really? Cause what I think is you are a heartless, cruel, ignorant jerk!" I snapped. Chase's face twisted with pain.

"Would you just listen, and let me explain?" His voice trembled with anger and shame.

"No, I don't want to hear your lame, well-rehearsed explanation. I thought you were the same sweet boy who wouldn't hurt a fly, but I was wrong, because you've changed. Stay away from me." With that, I stormed up to the house.

I showered, got changed into something warmer, and grabbed my guitar case. As I walked out onto the sandy path, I saw that Chase hadn't left his spot on the beach. He was sitting in the sand; head in hands, letting the wind toss his hair around.

I didn't need him.

Chase's Point of View:

Never have I ever fucked up so badly. Never have I ever hurt a girl so badly. Sure, I've done some pretty mean things to past girls, but nothing compared to this.

Hayden wasn't like other girls. She didn't wear bucket loads of makeup, or listen to crappy pop music. She had a sense of humor, compassion, and knew how to have a good time. She was real, she was special, she was different.

I cared about her, I always have. She grew up with me, knew me better than anyone else. But most of all, I could be myself around her.

But what I did … that wasn't me. That was Chase, the super hot lifeguard whose got a rep for playing girls - not Chase, the beach loving guy who is secretly afraid of getting hurt and becoming vulnerable.

And my biggest fear had occurred. Hayden, the only person who I had ever really cared about and opened up to, wanted nothing to do with me. It was my fault, not Tyler's, not Jessica's. I could have said "no" to the bet; I could have said "maybe next time." But, even they didn't know the real me, so I had to put on my alter ego and accept the challenge.

I wanted to fix this. I needed to fix this. Not sure how, but I will.

CHAPTER 11

Hayden's Point of View:

Mist and fog hovered over the Pier. People were bundled up in winter coats and scarves, unaccustomed to the below 70 weather (they would never survive through a Connecticut winter.)

I was strolling through the crowd, when the lead singer of a street performing band caught my eye.

Carmen, the waitress, was belting out some Janis Joplin. Her voice was incredible - raspy, soulful - and her vocal range was mind-boggling.. When she saw me watching, she indicated for me to come forward.

When the song finished, Carmen leaned forward and whispered, "Get out your quitar."

Of course, the one day I carry my guitar in public, I get swooped up into a street performing band. Can you say coincidence? Here comes the conflict - I have super stage fright. Its one thing performing in front of a few people, and another performing in front of a large crowd filled with strangers. But considering this day couldn't get any worse, I agreed. It was also sort of a self-deeming goal; if I could face my biggest fear, I could also face heartbreak, if I could get over my biggest fear, I could also get over Chase.

After pulling out my guitar, I quickly made sure it was in tune.

"What are we playing?" I whispered to the male guitarist, standing next to me.

"Like A Rolling Stone," he whispered back. "C chord, F chord …"

"Yeah, yeah," I cut him off. "I know the song." I heard him chuckle, but I was too preoccupied by my knotting stomach to respond.

When I heard the beat begin, I shut my eyes and strummed the first chord. Opening my eyes, I looked down at my guitar neck, checking my finger position. By the time, I looked back up; I was too into the song to care about the large crowd. When the song filled my ears, it killed my nerves - funny how music has that kind of power over me.

The song ended, leaving me with this surge of adrenaline and ecstasy, making me feel weightless and carefree. The crowd's applause only fueled me more. By the end of the set list, the crowd had faded out.

While packing up, Carmen said, "Thanks for joining us. You really added to the sound! I didn't know you were such a guitar goddess."

"Well, I wouldn't call myself that," I said, modestly. "You were the goddess. Where did you learn to sing like that?"

"Now, it's my turn to be modest," Carmen said, with a white smile. "So, what are you doing tonight? Cause there is a big party tonight, and you should come."

I thought of Chase's invitation to be his date to the party. "Oh yeah, I heard about that."

"Yeah, it's supposed to be huge," Carmen said. Going to a big party meant meeting plenty of new people and showing Chase that I didn't need him.

"Sure, why not!"

"Great, I'll pick you up around seven! You're staying at Chase Levine's house, right?"

I clenched my jaw before saying, "Yup."

"Cool, I know where his house is! See you then!" I watched her pack up the remaining equipment and hop into the band van.

Zipping up my guitar case, I started walking back to the house. If I wanted to show Chase what he was missing, I had to look HOT.

Back at the house, Rebecca and my mother were preparing dinner. John and Dad were watching a baseball game. Chase was nowhere in sight.

"Dinner in five minutes," Rebecca said. "Would you mind getting Chase? He's in his room."

"Sure," I said, with a fake smile. Leaving the kitchen, I walked to my bedroom and dropped my guitar case onto my bed. Then, I headed down the hallway to Chase's room.

A sad Don Mclean song was seeping through Chase's closed door. Invading his privacy, I swung it open.

"Asshole, dinners ready," I said. Turning on my heel, I headed into the dinning room.

The parents were already seated at the dinning table. I took the empty seat between Rebecca and my father. Dolefully, Chase slumped into a seat across the table. Under his sweatshirt hood, I could see his hair was tangled and his face was red.

"So how's everything going so far, Hayden? Do you like it here?" Rebecca asked, making dinner conversation.

"Yeah, I love it! California is absolutely beautiful. Plus, everyone here is super nice and kindhearted," I said, with a touch of sarcasm that only Chase would pick up on. And I knew he did, by the way he angrily slopped more mashed potatoes on his plate.

"Oh that's good! Meet any new friends?"

"Yeah! Chase introduced me to his friends Tyler and Jessica, who are just the sweetest people ever," I said, continuing to torment Chase with my sarcasm.

"Ex-girlfriend Jessica?" Rebecca asked Chase.

"Yup," he groaned.

"How nice," Rebecca said. By the tone of her voice, I could tell that she wasn't too fond of Jessica either. "Anyone else?"

"Yeah, this girl Carmen," I said. Turning to my mom, I said, "Which reminds me, can I go to a party with her tonight?"

Chase perked up, and shot me a confused look.

"A party? I'm not sure . . ." she said, being her normal, overprotective self.

"Stacy, relax, let the girl have her fun," Rebecca said. "Is this the same party Chase is going to?"

I was about to nod my head, when Chase said, "I don't think I'm going anymore."

"Why not?" I asked, even though I knew the answer. But in all honesty, I wanted him to go. I wanted him to see me dressed up. I wanted him to see that I could have a great time without him. I wanted him to see me flirting with other guys. I wanted him to get jealous.

"Just not in the mood." His eyes narrowed down at mine. For the first time today, I looked right back into his eyes and saw . . . pain, sorrow, weakness, guilt. Ache filling my heart, I looked away.

"May I be excused? I have to go get ready," I said. My mother nodded and told me to clear my plate. I did, then headed to my room.

Decisions, decisions. What to wear, what to wear. I settled on an aqua, Tiffany's Box blue tank and a tight grey skirt. Leaving my naturally wavy hair, I rimmed my eyes with black liner. Adding final touches, I slipped on black heels and my leather jacket. Carmen rang the doorbell just as I was taking one last look in the mirror; perfect timing.

Before answering the door, I peeked into Chase's room. Chase was spread out on his bed, throwing a tennis ball against the ceiling.

"Look, I'm heading to the party now," I said. Puzzled, Chase sat up, and stopped the throwing the ball. His eyes widened when he saw my outfit. "Don't let me stop you from going."

Adding a swing to my hips, I walked out and went towards the front door. As I passed the living room, John gave me a thumbs up.

"Hey girl," Carmen said, after I opened the door. "Ready to go?"

Smiling deviously with excitement, I closed the door behind me. Gracefully, I skipped down the stairs and into the passenger seat of her Jeep. Getting pumped, we blasted some loud music until we got to the party - home to loud music, lights, and hundreds of cars.

Arms linked, Carmen and I bounced over to the crowd of people. Everybody was either socializing, dancing, or drinking.

"Can I get you something to drink?" A random, decent looking guy asked.

"I'm good," I said politely. I wasn't really into that kind of stuff, you know drinking, smoking, etc. I wasn't straight edge, I just never saw the appeal of having no control of my actions, and then puking or feeling shitty later.

"Come on. At least take a beer or something." His breath reeked of alcohol.

"I'm good, thank you," I said, my tone growing firmer. Trying to send him the message to leave, I looked around the party. Over on the other side of the party, I saw Chase, standing alone, drinking out of a red cup.

"Last offer, you sure?" He said.

Seeing Chase made me change my mind. Maybe, just a little wouldn't hurt. Maybe, just a little would loosen me up a bit. "Actually, I'll take a beer."

A few minutes later, the guy came back with an unopened bottle of Bud light. Taking a large gulp, the beer made me cringe. It tasted like soap mixed with wheat and piss. Trying again, I took another sip - not as bad the second time.

You know how I said "just a little?" Well, that didn't really work out. An hour into the party, I was already downing tequila shots. I switched from a beer to a vodka twist. Sub-consciously, I knew I was going over board, but I couldn't stop. I was having fun! Guys were talking to me, flirting with me, asking for my number.

One guy in particular, caught my attention. His name was Dean. He had dark shaggy hair, bright green eyes, and wore a leather jacket similar to mine.

"Hey, you want to go upstairs for a bit?" He whispered in my ear. Eagerly, I nodded. Dean grabbed my hand and led me through the house, up the stairs, and into a random bedroom.

Before I knew it, I was lying on the bed, and Dean was on top of me. His tongue was exploring my mouth, as the alcohol in his breath filled my nostrils.

"Dean," I yelped. "What are you doing?" He didn't answer. Everything seemed so fuzzy and out of place. My eyes started swirling, and my stomach started churning.

Dean's hands started to roam around my body. With all his force, he attempted to pull my skirt off.

"Dean, stop!" I ordered. But again, he didn't listen, let alone answer. He started to remove his shirt, then his pants, then his boxers.

"I want to leave!" I shouted, trying to get out of his grasp, but he held me down onto the bed. Hopeless, I began to scream - loud, blood curling shrieks.

Dean grabbed a pillow, and tried to smother my mouth with it. But he wasn't fast enough, because someone had already barged in, and attacked Dean. My vision was too blurred to see who my hero was. The two of them were on the floor, throwing punches, beating the shit out of each other. With my chance to escape, I did . . . to the bathroom.

Dropping onto the tiled floor, I leaned over the toilet and puked, several times. Exhausted from the vomiting, I laid onto the cool, bathroom floor and gently closed my eyes.

I heard a familiar voice, but I didn't open my eyes. "Ace, you're going to be okay. I'm here, don't worry, I'll take care of you."

CHAPTER 12

I woke up in my own bed, still dressed in my party outfit. A killer headache, dizziness, and nausea greeted me. The pain caused me to groan.

"Oh you're up." I turned my head to the side to see Chase in the old rocking chair. The pillow behind his head and the blanket on his lap told me that he had spent the night in the chair.

"Yeah," I moaned. Pressing my hand against my forehead, I massaged my throbbing temple.

"Here take one of these," Chase said, getting up and handing me some Advil tablets. "What exactly do you remember from last night?"

"Well . . ." I started, trying to focus my fuzzy memory. "I remember drinking, a lot. And then going upstairs with some guy . . ."

"And . . ." Chase pushed me to think farther, but my brain wouldn't allow it.

"That's it. I'm drawing a blank from there." Chase got up from the rocking chair, and sat on the edge of my bed.

"Well, that guy tried to rape you. When I saw you go upstairs with him, I kept a close guard. I heard you scream so I barged in and pulled him off of you. While we were fighting, you must have crawled out to the bathroom. And that's where I found you, passed out."

"Well, thank you," I said, softly. My anger towards him started to melt.

Chase took a deep breath before saying, "Look Hayden, now that you're speaking to me, I've got to say a few things. I'm so incredibly sorry for what I did to you. The word 'sorry' doesn't even begin to express the pain, guilt, and remorse I feel. I know I can't justify what I did, but I have to tell you, that wasn't me. That was the jerk I pretend to be when I'm around my Californian friends. You're the only one of my friends that knows the real me, and the 'real Chase' would never do that."

"Chase, please," I said, the pounding in my head growing stronger.

"Hayden, I have to finish," Chase said, desperately. "You've always had a special place in my heart, Ace. And seeing you now, ten years later, the place has grown bigger. I don't want to be just friends anymore . . . I want to be more. I was hoping this summer was going to be our chance to finally get together, but this stupid bet screwed everything up. I wanted to kiss you, because I like and care about you, not because I wanted some cash. You've got to believe me, but I know you probably won't. Please, just let me show you that I do feel this way, give me a second chance."

So much to soak in, so much to process. His voice, his eyes, his words all showed truth in what he was saying. But, what if it happened again? What if I let my guard down, and history repeated itself?

"Chase, I want to believe you, but I'm afraid to. I'm not sure if I trust you anymore. I'm willing to give you that second chance, but you're going to have to earn my trust back. I don't want to know two sides of you, see your two faces. I want the real Chase, that I know and love. Please, don't let me down."

"I won't," he whispered, before pulling me into a tight embrace.

Still hungover, Chase insisted that I have a mental health day. He also insisted on staying home and taking care of me. Chase made Mac & Cheese (great hangover food) and tea, watched movies with me, and made sure I was always comfortable.

"Hey," Chase shook me awake. I had fallen asleep on his lap during the movie. "Come outside, you have to see this."

"Mom, five more minutes," I groaned, sleepily. I pulled the blanket over my head and rolled over on my side.

"No, no you'll miss it . . . don't make me do this," Chase playfully threatened.

"Go away," I said, desperate for sleep.

"Okay, you asked for it." Chase broke into a tickle attack. Squirming and giggling, I found myself fully awake now.

"You win," I said, standing up and wrapping the blanket around my shoulders. "But this better be worth it."

Chase led me outside onto the back porch, and told me to lie down and look at the sky. I did so, and he lied next to me. I gazed up at the sky, waiting to see what all the hype was about when ... a shooting star swam across. Then another, and another, and another, and another! I lost track of how many I saw.

"Meteor shower," Chase whispered. Fascinated by the sight, I smiled and squeezed his hand.

"This is amazing," I whispered back.

"Worth sparing a few minutes of sleep?"

"Definitely."

The next day, I woke up, feeling good as new. The sun was shining, a warm breeze was coming in from my bedroom window, and I could hear the loud croaks of the beach seagulls. Feeling energized, I got on my purple bikini, and covered up with a grey off-the-shoulder shirt.

I heard the shower running in Chase's bathroom. Skipping down the hallway, I headed to the kitchen, hoping to grab some breakfast. Rebecca left a note on the counter, letting us know they would be out for the day, however she didn't specify where.

Today, I felt invincible. The bad spell was over, everything was fixed. The reassurance that everything was okay between Chase and I filled me up with optimism. However, that optimism was crushed when the doorbell rang.

"Hello?" I swung open the door, and saw the vain of my existence. Literally, I had to stop myself from lunging towards them and ripping their hair out.

"Hey there," Tyler said, with an innocent smile. It disgusted me that he could act so perfectly normal, like nothing was wrong. "Is Chase around? Or did he already leave for work?"

"He's in the shower," I said, coldly.

"Okay, well I'll wait for him," Tyler said, barging in without permission. I guess he didn't need an invitation, seeing as this was his best friend's house. Smugly, he flopped onto the couch and put his bare feet on the coffee table. "So, what's cookin' good lookin'?"

How lame. "Cut the crap."

"Where did that come from? I was just being friendly," Tyler said.

"Oh is that what you call it? Was making a bet about me another friendly gesture?"

Tyler put on this face that made it seem like he was offended, however his eyes gave him away.

"Look, we were just messing around. It's what Chase and I do. We're guys, we're bros, it's just how our friendship is," Tyler said. "Don't take it personally."

"Wow, you really are a jerk. Don't take it personally? So, you've done this to other girls, which makes it so much better? If that's your thought process, then that just makes you a sick bastard. I hope you're really content with who you are, because once an ass, always an ass."

"Ouch, baby, you're harsh," Tyler said, with a smirk. "Who knew you were so feisty."

"Get over yourself," I said, tired of this, tired of him. Why was Chase friends with him? I know that deep down Chase was a good guy, but I couldn't help but worry that maybe Tyler was a bad influence on him.

Tyler got up from the couch, and walked towards me, taking his sweet time.

"Hayden, don't write me off as such a bad guy. I did it for you," Tyler said, trying to flip the story. "When you came here, you reconnected with Chase, your little 'childhood lover' which instantly closed yourself off from other guys. You never gave other guys, here in California, the chance." I started walking towards the kitchen, and Tyler followed me. "Guys like me. When I saw you, I couldn't get over how damn sexy you were. But I heard about your date with Chase, and how you guys looked at each other, and I knew I had to change that. So I made the bet with Chase, knowing you would find out and dump his ass. Originally, I was going to have Jessica tell you, but you waking up and seeing worked out even better. So you see, I did it for a good reason. I want you, Hayden. And when I want something, I get it."

He just dug himself in a huge hole. He was rude, cocky, arrogant, backstabbing, and selfish. Thinking fast, I grabbed the water bottle that was on the kitchen counter and emptied it on him. Tyler jerked back and wiped his drenched face of the water.

"Get this through your head. I, Hayden Peterson, will never ever get with you. Now, I'm going to let you slide on this, and not tell Chase what you did, but if you ever try to meddle with our relationship again, I will reveal whom you really are. I will also make sure that I contact each and every girl you've ever used or hurt, so that they can help me make your life a living hell." Just as I finished, I heard the shower turn off. "Now, go get Chase and get out of my sight before I decide to change my mind."

Tyler scattered off to Chase's room like a scared puppy. Proud of myself, I sat on the couch and soaked in my victory. A few minutes later, I heard Chase and Tyler voices echo through the house.

"Hey dude, I was just about to leave for work," I heard Chase say. "Why are you soaking wet?"

"It's a long story," I heard Tyler grumble. Their conversation was drowned by the sounds of the footsteps.

Wearing matching lifeguard trunks and sunglasses, the two of them looked like twins.

"Hey Ace," Chase said, leaning over the couch side. He went in for the kiss, but because of the trust issue, I turned my head to the side so his lips landed on my cheek. "We're going to go to work, but I'll be back later. Don't have too much fun without me."

"Okay, go guard some lives" I said, gazing sweetly at Chase, then shooting daggers with my eyes at Tyler. Looking to the ground, Tyler sheepishly avoided my glare.

After they left, I started thinking, maybe I had been too generous with Tyler. After all, he did hurt me, so why should I hurt him? But, as I thought more, two wrongs don't make a right. And there's this motto, kill your enemies with kindness. Not to mention, I could take in pride in the fact that I was a better person than Tyler - I mean why should I sink to his level?

I left for the beach, hoping to soak in some sun. However, I quickly got bored of tanning and swimming. Because I was having a positive, unbeatable day, I decided to make a bold decision and leaped towards a new experience.

"Hey," I said, approaching a friendly-looking cluster of surfers. "Do any of you know where I could find local surf lessons?"

An older, male, middle-aged surfer spoke. "Yeah, I know there's a teacher down on the West Beach, but he runs pretty expensive."

"Yeah, way too over priced," a young female said. "But you know, I'm pretty sure we all wouldn't mind teaching you for free?" She looked around for the group's approval. When she saw them nod, she continued. "We need another in the pack, so we can have an even number."

This was working out better than I planned. The people in California were much more benevolent than the people in Connecticut.

"Really? That'd be amazing, thank you!"

"No problem," one surfer, who I later found out was named Tim, said. "So, first, you'll need a board. Mark, you have an extra long board right?"

Mark, the older one who I first spoke to, nodded. He disappeared for a quick moment, then came back with an oversized tan and blue surfboard. The young female, who I later found out was named Casey, lent me a wetsuit.

From there, they taught me all the basic knowledge of surfing. I started by practicing my form on the sand, then in shallow water. I grasped the concept pretty quickly, and Mark told me I was a natural. By mid afternoon, they said I was ready to take my skill into deeper water and attempt to catch a wave.

It took a few tries, but eventually, I got up and started riding a wave. The adrenaline and rush was similar to the one I got when I was performing with Carmen and her street band. But, this had a different effect and connection. Instead of connecting with the music and notes, I connected with the wave and nature. The wind whipped through my hair, the water misted my skin - I was on top of the world . . . until I lost my balance. As if in slow motion, I started tumbling downwards, into the crashing current of the sea. My head went under the surface, and the sea violently tossed me around. Eventually, I felt my body wash upon the shore. Casey, Mark, and Tim caught up with me and helped me up.

"Are you okay? That was a nasty wipeout," Tim said.

"I'm . . . fine," I panted, the wind knocked out of me.

Casey grabbed my arm and pulled it close to your face. "Hayden, you're gushing blood."

She lifted my arm up, and I saw the red liquid oozing from my arm.

"It's just a scratch," I said, playing it off.

"No, I don't think so," Mark commented, while making a close examination. "It looks pretty deep. You should head to First Aid shack and get it check out."

Casey walked me over to the shack, where a few of the lifeguards were stationed. Among those lifeguards was Chase.

Chase's eyes brightened when he saw me, but they soon grew dark. Glancing from my trembling face, to my tangled hair, down to my wounded arm.

"Hayden, what happened to you?" He rushed over to me, sliding one arm behind my back and one hand on my face. Chase helped me down into a wooden chair.

"I . . . uh . . ." Starting to feel dizzy from the loss of blood, I couldn't finish my sentence.

"We were teaching her to surf, and she took a bad tumble," Casey reported.

Chase pressed a piece of antibacterial cloth onto my wound. With a cotton ball and anti-stringent, he wiped the blood away and cleaned the cut.

"It looks fairly deep," he said. "You're going to need a few stitches."

"Aw man," I moaned, my head spinning.

"I'll take you to the medical center," he said. Chase swooped me up into his arms, and carried me to his car. "Ace, you can close your eyes and rest. I'll wake you when we get there."

"Is this going to be a regular ritual? You saving the day, being my hero, taking care of me and junk?" I asked, softly.

"If you keep acting recklessly, it will. But hey, I could get used to this whole knight in shinning armor role," he said, with a playful tone. With a smile, I closed my eyes, knowing I was in good hands.

CHAPTER 14

As always, the hospital was a drag. While I was getting stitched up, Chase filled out the papers and called our parents to let them know what happened.

"How do you feel?" Chase asked, after my arm was repaired.

"Just spiffy," I said, sarcastically. I tugged at the bandage tightly wrapped around my arm.

"Superb," he said. "Let's get out of here." Slowly, I got out of the white sheet bed and wobbled along.

When we entered the waiting room, Chase handed the nurse the clipboard with the necessary files.

"Thanks, Mr. Levine," the nurse said. "How's your father doing?"

"My father?" Chase asked, confused.

"Yeah, he was just in today, for some tests. I hope he's feeling better," she said, unaware of the misconception.

"Oh, yeah," Chase said. His eyes narrowed, while his jaw clenched. After we left, I got the sense that Chase didn't want to talk. He was obviously baffled and thrown off by what the nurse said.

Actually, I didn't mind the silence in the car ride home. It gave me time to just to swim in my pool of thoughts and memories. And, there's something special about our relationship, that Chase and I didn't need words, didn't need to talk. Sometimes, people feel awkward when a conversation isn't flowing. But, that wasn't the case. No need for words, our minds and souls communicated.

By the time we got home, the pain killers began to wear off. Silently, Chase handed me the prescription the doctor gave me. I went into the kitchen, greeted by my panicking parents.

"Hayden! God, you've had us worried! Are you okay? What happened?"

"I'm fine," I said, grabbing a water bottle and swallowing my pills. "It's just a scratch, a few stitches. I'll be fine."

Chase stomped into the kitchen, and slammed his backpack on the floor.

"So, when were you guys going to tell me about Dad? Or were you just going to hide it from me?" There was anger and pain mixed in his voice. A different kind of pain and hurt, than I had caused him.

"Oh, no," Rebecca cried. She ran over to him, and petted his hair. "Baby, we were going to tell you, but we needed to find the right time."

He pushed her off. "Sooner rather than later? What would have been the right time? When he was in his death bed? I can't believe you guys would lie to me like this."

"Chase," John's voice bellowed. "I know you're angry, but let's go for a walk and talk about it."

Chase looked at the ground, as John slipped an arm around his shoulders. They walked out the back door.

"Mom, Rebecca?" My voice sounded younger and more innocent, as if I was a young, scared child. "What's going on?"

Rebecca indicted that I should sit on the counter stool. "Sweetie, John's sick. You see, he's been feeling under the weather for quite a while now. And, his family has had a past with cancer. So, we've been running some tests lately, and the results keep coming back positive."

My stomach dropped. Uncle John? Young, energetic, healthy, funny Uncle John was sick? My head started spinning. No, no, it couldn't be. He couldn't have cancer, it wasn't possible. "What . . . kind of cancer?"

"Kidney. It hasn't started spreading, but it's getting close. He's going to go under treatment soon, to prevent spreading and hopefully destroy the cancer."

"So, he's going to be okay, right?" I asked, trying to be optimistic and looking for some hope.

"It's too soon to tell yet," Rebecca said softly, tears streaming out of her eyes. My mother placed a comforting hand on my shoulder.

"I need to go outside for a bit, get some fresh air and clear my head," I said. Slowly, I hopped down from my chair, and headed out to the back porch. Spreading myself onto the lounge couch, I rested my head on my hands and elevated my feet.

I wished that these tests were wrong, that some error had occurred, but I knew that wasn't likely. I wished that Uncle John would fight and recover quickly, but I knew that wasn't likely either.

Uncle John didn't deserve this. He was the greatest man, husband, father, and friend. He always did the right thing, showed unmeasured kindness, and went out of his way to make anyone feel better.

Not to mention, I regretted not spending more time with him. Spending almost a month here, I didn't even think to hang out with him. I had to change that, God only knows how much time we had left before he . . .

After soaking in my thoughts, Chase and John walked up. Chase looked upset, his cheeks were flushed and his lips were curled into a scowl. John patted Chase on the back, before heading inside. I sat up, pulled my knees to my chest. Chase slumped over and sat on the couch. He stared at the ground.

"Hey, come here." I wrapped my arms around him, pulling him into a tender hug. He buried his face into my chest. We sat there, hugging for a while. Once again, we didn't need words. We just needed to hold each other.

"I don't know what's going to happen. I'm scared, Hayden." I put my finger to his lips, showing him that he didn't need to speak because I understood.

"You're going to be okay, he's going to be okay. We'll get through this," I whispered, still holding onto him. "Now, it's my turn to take care of you."

CHAPTER 15

15 movies, 5 tubs of ice cream, 2 blankets, 1 couch, 2 pizzas, 3 bags of Swedish Fish, 4 days.

Day to night, sunrise to sunset, Chase and I spent every minute wallowing. Although it was far from productive, it was really the best cure of sadness. Sometimes, you just need to take a break from your life.

When we weren't watching movies, we were bonding with Uncle John. We played cards, talked about interesting topics, and looked through old photo albums. Once John started treatment, we wouldn't be able to do these things with him anymore.

The days passed, and I knew it was time to reconnect with the outside world. However, I didn't want to push or force Chase to do anything he wasn't ready for. The emotional healing process was a delicate path, full of prepared baby steps.

"Hey, I was thinking, maybe we could get some fresh air today and take a walk on the beach...the sun's setting and it's really pretty..." I trailed off. "You up for it?"

"I don't know, Ace," Chase said, weakly. His usual bright eyes were now pale and lifeless.

"Come on, just a little stroll won't hurt, right?" I smiled hopefully, my eyes beaming up at him.

"Okay," he muttered, giving into my angelic and promising expression. We got up and changed out of our pajamas. I slipped on some jeans, cuffed them mid calf, and threw on a sweatshirt, making sure to be careful of my stitches. Chase was wearing a similar outfit, in cargo shorts and an American Apparel hoodie.

Leaving the house for the first time in days was refreshing. Vegetating is good, but all in moderation. At some point, you have to get up and try to continue on with life, or else you'll be stuck in that phase forever.

The beach was nearly empty, only a handful of people were still lingering around. Chase and I held hands as we strolled down the beach, collecting smooth shells. At this moment, the beach was absolutely perfect. The remainder of the sun gave off the last bit of warmth, before the nasty winds kicked in. The waves were forceful, as their sounds gently echoed in my ears. Above the water line, the sky was painted beautiful oranges and pinks. This sight almost made me sad, in the way that it was too beautiful - it didn't fit in with the rest of the cruel and ugly world. I wondered if Chase felt the same way.

We strolled past the First Aid and Lifeguard Shack, and my injured arm itched with the painful memory. Chase said he wanted to stop by and check in with everyone, so we changed the direction of our walk and dropped by.

Most of the lifeguards were still there, even though it was way past their working hours. All of the guys, including Tyler, greeted Chase and asked what was going on with him lately. However, I noticed Chase had this way of avoiding what was really happening, because he'd reply with "everything's fine, just needed a break" or "just some family stuff, it'll work out."

He said his goodbyes, and we continued down with our walk. Until Tyler ran over and interrupted it . . .

"Bro," he said, once he caught up to us. "What's really going on with you?"

I looked up at Chase, whose face twisted in agony. "Nothing, it's not a big deal."

"Look, you don't miss numerous days of work for nothing."

"Tyler, I don't want to talk about it, okay?" I could tell that Chase was getting rather annoyed.

"Okay, cool. Don't tell your best friend!" Tyler growled. "Does she know?"

"Hey, don't drag me into this," I snapped.

"Tyler, back off okay?" Chase said, taking a step in front of me.

"No, I wont. Dude, you've been acting differently lately. Ever since she came! I feel like I don't even know you," Tyler spat.

Before I knew it, Chase had punched Tyler square in the jaw, causing Tyler to fall to his knees. Quickly recovering, Tyler hopped up and threw a punch. From there, the shoving began, and the fight grew more intense and violent.

I managed to squeeze in between the two of them. When they saw it was me, they immediately stopped. Despite the fact that they were both panting and bleeding, their eyes showed that they weren't finished.

I glared at Tyler before saying, "Let's go, Chase."

Silently, I helped Chase walk back to the house. I went into the kitchen, and pulled out an icepack, as well a damp cloth.

Handing the icepack to Chase, and dabbing his cuts, I said, "I'm sorry. Maybe it's too early to go out and interact with people."

Chase's dropping eyes looked into mine. "No, it's my fault. Tyler was just really pissing me off. He has been for a while."

"But that doesn't mean you should result to fighting! You could have gotten really hurt. Plus, if more people saw, you could have gotten in big trouble.

"I know, I know. I just don't know what came over me," he said, disappointed in himself.

"Just … be careful, okay?" I said, wiping the last bit of blood away. I held his face in my hands, taking one last examination, before kissing him softly on the lips. It had been the first time we had kissed since the boat, but since then, Chase had proved himself worthy of my trust.

Chase slipped his hands into my hair, and pulled me closer to him. His body was pressed up against mine, and our arms wrapped around each other.

Forgiveness is difficult because it requires a full acceptance of the issue and truly moving on. Trust is hard to earn, and even harder to regain. And second chances cannot be free tickets to not be accounted for one's faults. But somehow, Chase had overcome all of these struggles. And that alone, deserved some kind of reward.

Knowing we shouldn't push it, we stopped kissing. Continuing our tradition, we snuggled on the couch, while debating what movie to watch.

"Wait!" An idea just popped into my head. I hurried into my bedroom, dug to the bottom of my suitcase of random crap, and pulled out a plastic DVD case. My eyes widen with excitement.

Walking back into the living room, I held the DVD cover in front of my face.

"No way, not happening," Chase said, shaking his head when he saw what it was.

"Why not! Trust me, I know you'll love it!"

"No, I wont. If I watch that, I swear my balls will fall off. I'd rather not lose my masculinity," Chase rebutted.

"Please? Give it a try, for me?" I put on my best pouty face. But he continued to shake his head. I kissed him on his cheek, then his lips, then his forehead, then his ear. He was about to kiss me back, when I pulled away and said, "Nope, you can't kiss me, until you agree to watch it!"

Chase frowned. "I hate that you have this power over me. Fine, we can watch it, but only the first disc, and then we're done."

I kissed him, and let him kiss me back. Bouncing up, I put Disc 1 of the Vampire Diaries into the DVD player.

For both of us, this was a brand new experience. I had never watched the show, just read the books. But my friend back at home bought me the first series as a going-away gift.

Well, we watched the first disc. And then the second. And then the third. 9 hours of pure goodness.

Chase declared he was Team Damon, while I disagreed and said I was Team Stefan. I was proud to say that Chase was equal, maybe even more into the show than I was.

"How's that masculinity doing?" I asked, when he got up to change the disc. Chase sat back down, and I rested my head in his lap.

"Hey this is pretty masculine. I'm digging all the blood and violence," Chase said, trying to justify his love for the show.

"I knew you'd love it, I totally called it," I said. After reading the digital clock (4:27) under the television, my eyes began to close.

"Yeah, yeah you were right," I heard Chase said, but I was too tired to respond. "You sleep, Ace. I'd be more than happy to re-watch the episodes with you tomorrow."

Before lowering the volume slightly, he lightly kissed my forehead. He pulled the blanket higher over me, and I wrapped my arm around his waist. As I had multiple times before, I let myself fall asleep in his warm and comfortable embrace.

CHAPTER 16

Things got better around the house. And when John start-ed chemotherapy, it had a surprisingly good effect. It pushed us out of any sort of denial we were still in, and reassured us that John was getting help.

Chase was feeling that much better that he was ready to go back to work. I knew I should have been happy for him, being able to take that big step, but I couldn't help but worry. Lately, Chase had been really sensitive and easily infuriated, especially around Tyler. I knew it was just his way of coping and it would soon pass, but that didn't stop my paranoia.

Chase was working today and the parents were out, which meant I had the whole house to myself. Feeling trapped and lonely in the big empty house, I decided to go out shopping. I was just about to leave when the doorbell rang. Grabbing my bag and Chase's car keys, I answered it.

I swung open the door, and hunched over. "Chase isn't here right now, you can come back later."

"Actually," Jessica's high pitched voice said. "I'm here to see you. Can we talk?"

Thrown off by this, I said, "I'm sorry, now isn't the best time. I was just about to leave."

"Please, Hayden, it will only take a few minutes," she said in desperation.

"Okay," I said, standing aside so she could step inside.

Her stilettos clonked along the wooden floor. She dropped her expensive-looking purse (one that pitied my hemp, over the shoulder bag) on the couch, and sat down.

"I'm really sorry for everything, Hayden. The day you got here, I personally singled you out, because you were competition. Chase dumped me in May, but we decided to stay good friends, even though I continuously persuaded him and tried to win him back. When he found out you were staying for the summer, he constantly talked about how excited he was to see you again, and I let my jealousy take the best of me," Jessica said, almost in tears.

"Jessica . . ." I said, practically speechless.

"I'm not done yet. Seeing you as a newcomer, I seized the chance to victimize and take you down. I threatened you, but that wasn't enough. Tyler confronted me with the idea to make the bet, to ruin your relationship with Chase. It was a win-win deal for the two of us. I would get Chase, he would get you. But, I felt sick afterwards because it was cruel and low-leveled. I want to apologize for everything, and tell you that I really admire you, for being so strong. You handled all of your problems – Tyler, me, Chase, his father – so beautifully and with class. And I can tell you're really good for Chase. He needs someone as kind and attentive and smart and beautiful and affectionate as you."

"Well thank you," I said, still speechless. After a few minutes of awkward silence I said, "I guess I can go shopping later. Do you want to stay for a bit?"

Jessica nodded. I got up, asked if she wanted anything to drink, and she politely declined.

"So, why the apology all of a sudden?" I asked, finally addressing the subject.

"I've wanted to for a while now. Today just seemed like a good time to do it," she said. "I'm really glad I did, because I just want to put this in the past and hope that we can be friends."

I walked out of the kitchen and sat next to her on the couch.

"Jessica, it was really noble of you to apologize, but that doesn't erase or justify what you did. You really hurt me, and its going to take more than a 'sorry' to make it up. I can tell you really mean it and you feel guilty, but that doesn't make up for the damage you've done. What I'm trying to say is that I accept your apology and I'd like to move on, but it's not going to be all sunshine and butterflies. I don't exactly trust you. Lately, I've been struggling with trust. Unlike other people, I initially trust a person. However, if that person does something to lose my trust, it's not easily given back. You have to work to re-earn my trust, and prove yourself to me. Just like Chase, I'm willing to give you a second chance, or in this case a clean slate, but you're going to have to earn my trust back."

After the words left my mouth, I realized how blunt and painfully honest they were. I know I probably offended her in some way, but I couldn't let myself become a doormat, giving her the opportunity to just walk all over me.

"I understand," she said, dolefully. We sat in silence for a while, till she spoke again. "Hayden, why do you keep giving out second chances and forgiveness? Tyler told me what you did for him, not ratting him out to Chase. And obviously, you forgave Chase."

I thought about this for a while. Why did I do this? Why show sympathy to those who didn't deserved it?

"I don't really know. I mean, in life we're all going to make mistakes, but why should be penalized to such a degree? If someone is truly sorry for what they did and learned their lesson, they should be given the chance to make it up, and prove that they've changed. I'm willing to do that, if they know that they aren't easily off the hook and their wont be that third chance. And it's like baseball, you know three strikes. You do it the first time, strike. You do It the second time, strike. You do it the third time, you're out, game over, you're done. In my book, the second strike puts you on the line, because I'm willing to forgive, but not forget."

Jessica sat there, enamored. "Wow, Hayden. I don't think I could ever be like that, like you. You're honestly a saint. If I was in your position, I would have wanted revenge. You're such a good person, and I'm just a monster," her voice trembled, as tears streamed down her face, ruining her mascara. I slipped my arm around her.

"Jessica, you can do that. Learn that revenge doesn't solve anything. Two wrongs don't make a right – an eye for an eye only makes the world blind. Deep down, I know you're a good person who makes bad decisions. A bad person wouldn't have come here today and apologized for their actions, a good person would have," I said, trying to reassure her. "Come on, let's go wash your face with some cool water."

Heading to the bathroom, we splashed water on her face until she felt better.

"Can I apologize for another thing?" Jessica asked, once we were back on the couch. I nodded for her to proceed. "I want to apologize for Tyler's behavior. It would be better coming from him, but he's too damn proud to admit his mistakes. Tyler can be really arrogant and selfish, but he's got a good heart. You should see him around kids, it's one of the sweetest things. But, you should know, that I've never seen him so love sick over one girl. Tyler doesn't date, doesn't love, doesn't even care about most girls, but you seem to be the exception. It may be sick and cruel, but this is his way of showing he cares about you."

This was a perfect example of how I couldn't trust her. If she hadn't betrayed me, I could assume that she was telling the truth. But, far as I know, this could have been another trick.

"Strange," I said, trying to avoid continuing the conversation.

Jessica sensed my the tension. "Well I should get going." She gathered her things and headed towards the front door. "See you around. And, thank you."

My lips curled into a warm yet small smile. "You're welcome."

When I closed my door, I felt a sudden urge and need to tell someone what happened. Screw shopping, I needed to vent!

Pulling out my cell phone, I dialed Carmen. "Hey are you free right now? I really need to talk to someone."

"I'm working right now, but come over anyway, and I'll just take my break," Carmen said, brightly.

"I'll be right over!"

Rushing, I headed for the pier, hyped on the feeling that I was going to burst soon if I didn't talk about what happened. Pushing through the crowd of people loitering on the Pier, I made my way to the Sandy Shell. It wasn't dinner rush hour yet, so I was able to waltz right into the restaurant.

Spotting Carmen, I pulled her over and let my mouth run off. She sat there patiently, listening closely, and waiting till I was done to speak.

"Holy shit," she said. "Who knew!"

"Dude, I need you say more than that, I'm dying! I have no idea what to think about this," I said, exasperated.

"I think that Jessica never fails to surprise me, but who knows. Keep close tabs on her, and see how things play out. As for Tyler … well I'm not really sure. But you should confront him about it, about everything, because things need to be sorted out. If he does really like you, we've got problems because he's a mad trickster, who doesn't listen to anybody but himself. If he doesn't like you, then we've also got problems, because that means Jessica and him are up to something, contradicting everything that happened." Shit, she was good. Obviously, I had chosen the right person to vent to.

"But when?"

"How about right now. He's sitting right over there," she pointed towards the bar, where Tyler sitting. I must have been so out of control and pre-occupied that I didn't even notice him when I walked in. "When he's not working, partying, or fucking girls, he's here 'supporting the family business.'"

Fully energized by the situation, I marched up to him and tapped him on the shoulder. He swung around to face me, and brightened up.

"What's your deal? Do you like me or do you not? Am I just this girl who you have an ultimate conquest for, or do you actually want to get to know me? Or am I just another victim for some stupid competition? Is that it? Are you trying to prove to Chase that you're better than him? That you can get more girls? Steal his girls? Is that what it is? I don't even know who you are! Are you this player who feels the need to be jerk or are you this sweet guy who loves to play with kids? Are you a loyal or backstabbing friend? Answer me in one word." Low on air, I huffed. Tapping my foot, I waited impatiently for my answer.

Quickly, Tyler grabbed hold of me, pulled me close, and kissed me. My entire body relaxed, not aware of what was happening. When I came to my realization, I pushed him off.

"I don't kiss girls, they kiss me. That should answer your questions," he said, before walking away.

CHAPTER 17

Unintentionally, my fingers touched my lips, leaving me stunned at what had happened. Tyler, the dick, the player, the best friend of Chase, had kissed me, the new girl, the outsider, the girlfriend of Chase.

Tyler hadn't answered a single question; he had only created more.

Carmen rushed over to me. "What the fuck just happened?"

"I don't know," I said, dumbfounded. Slowly coming back to life, I strunged the events together to explain what happened.

"So Jessica wasn't lying," Carmen said, shaking her head distastefully.

"How do you know that?" I asked. For some reason, today I couldn't stop questioning everything.

"Because Tyler doesn't kiss girls. His player technique is luring the girl in but making them initiate the first move. That way, when he leaves the girl, she can only blame herself for being 'too forward.'"

"But he kissed me?" I said.

"Right, which means you're not just another regular girl that he's going to use and then throw out like a tissue. It means that he's really into you. It means he's not pulling his usual player method on you. It means he's jeopardizing his friendship with Chase, for a girl he can't resist."

"No, no," I said, denying it. "It can't be! Something must be wrong, must be off. It's got to be some kind of trick or something."

"Tyler wouldn't dare ruin his reputation as a player for some sort of trick. And even if it was some sort of ploy, it was still to win you over."

Weakness shivered through my legs, and my stomach began to churn. "I think I'm going to be sick." I fell onto a chair, and took deep breaths. "Why would he do this to Chase?"

"Because Tyler is a selfish guy, who does whatever it takes to get what he wants, even if it means hurting his best friend," Carmen said, speaking in a calm and soothing voice.

"That's horrible! He's horrible!" I started crying from all the stress and confusion. "What about Chase? What do I do, what do I say? He's going to take this so badly, I know he is! And he's either going to dump me or dump Tyler!"

"Shhh," Carmen cooed, as she pulled me into an embrace. "It's going to be okay. You have to tell Chase exactly what happened, everything from the bet to Jessica's apology to the kiss. He'll understand, and he's not going to dump you. But, most likely he will stop being friends with Tyler. You can't cover for him again, he deserves it this time."

Yes, Tyler did deserve this. I had protected him once, and warned him to never try again. And yet, he did so anyway. He betrayed me, and even worst, he betrayed Chase. Chase needed to know the truth, that Tyler was a backstabbing, girlfriend stealing, friend. Tyler didn't deserve Chase's friendship, and yet I couldn't help but feel bad for Tyler. Maybe deep down, he was a good guy who made bad decisions, like Jessica. But reality was, Tyler needed to change, and he had to suffer for his consequences, and learn from his mistakes.

Carmen drove me home, knowing I was too upset to make the walk back. The tears had stopped, but the uneasy and sick feeling had not. Nevertheless, the moment I walked through the door and saw Chase sitting on the couch with a big smile, the water works came back.

Running over to Chase, I curled up next to him, and sobbed into his chest. Chase didn't ask questions, which I was thankful for. He just let me cry, while he stroked my hair and soothed me.

When I was all cried out, I sat up. Following Carmen's instructions, I told him everything, filling in my opinion along the way.

"I see," he said, uncomfortable. "Well he obviously likes you, no doubt about it. The question is . . . do you like him?"

"NO!" I blurted out. Knowing I was talking far too fast, I continued. "I don't want you to ever think that. I could care less if he liked me, honestly I don't know why he does. But, I think he's a player, vile, egotistical, self-centered, greedy, heartless, and spoiled. Other girls might fall for him, but not me! I don't love him, I love you!"

Now, I had really done it. I instantly regretted saying those three little words. Yes, I was sure of my feelings, because since we were kids, I loved him. Seeing him this summer and being with him, only confirmed and strengthened my feelings, taking them to a whole new level. But I thought it was far too early in our relationship to admit our feelings. And once you say it, you can never take it back.

Chase stared at me for a moment, which made me nervous. Honestly, I had no idea what was running through his head right now.

Finally he said, "I love you too, Hayden. I always have."

Tears ran down my face, in utter joy and relief. Today had been a rough, frustrating and drama filled day - but right now, all of my problems seemed so far away.

Chase kissed me, softly and tenderly. "Please, don't cry. I can't stand to see you sad."

"I'm not sad anymore," I said, laughing through the tears. "Words cannot describe the happiness I feel right now."

I kissed him back. Still kissing, we moved as one, heading in the direction of the bedrooms - we both were thinking the same thing. It was time; the perfect and right time.

Going into Chase's bedroom, we flopped onto his bed. Chase removed his shirt, and placed himself onto of me. He helped me remove my shirt, revealing my bra.

"Are you sure you want to do this?" Chase asked, before removing his pants.

"Positive. If there's anyone I want to lose it to, it's you. I'm ready."

"And it's not because you feel bad about what happened with Tyler and you think this is the only way to prove to me that you love me?"

"Mood killer!" I exclaimed, with a playful laugh. "I don't need to prove anything to you, because you know how I really feel about you. Look into my eyes, and tell me what do you see when I look at you?"

"I see . . . love." He looked down at me, with a comforting grin spread across his face.

My smile was all he needed to know that it was okay to proceed. The first surge of pain turned into pleasure. Our bodies, minds, hearts, souls connected as one - only resulting in a whole new degree of love.

When it's right, there's no doubts, regrets, or second thoughts. When it's right, you know that the person eternally loves you as much as you love them. When it's right, the wait is worth it, even if it means waiting seventeen years for the right guy.

Chapter 18

The next morning, I felt Chase begin to stir.

"Good morning," Chase whispered, kissing my ear. I moaned, not willing to get up, let alone open my eyes. I felt him remove his arm from my waist and sit up. "Go back to sleep."

Forcing my eyes open, I held his arm tightly. "Please, stay."

"How can I say no to you?" Chase said, resuming his position. He pulled me up, so that my head rested on his bare chest. He stroked my hair, trying to soothe me back to sleep.

But knowing he was awake, waiting on me, made it nearly impossible to return to my deep sleep. So, I enjoyed the cuddling for a little bit longer, before getting up.

"I'll go start breakfast," Chase said, leaving me to my thoughts.

Last night seemed surreal. It was magical, passionate, and memorable. I had lost my virginity to Chase, the guy I loved, and nothing was more powerful than that. And I knew that it was a little early . . . after all, he had just re-earned my trust the other day. But trust isn't measured in time – hours, days, weeks, months, years – it is measured in emotions and value.

I threw something on to cover myself, then headed into the kitchen, where Chase was cooking breakfast.

"A man in the kitchen," I said, as I entered. "What a pleasant twist to the stereotype."

Chase looked up at me and laughed. "A woman dressed only in a man's button down. What a delightful cliché."

"Touché."

Chase flipped two blueberry pancakes onto a clean plate, and handed it to me. Eagerly, I took a greedy bite. Buttery goodness and blueberry flavor wooed my taste buds.

"Mmmm, you put the Iron Chefs to shame," I said. Chase smiled, as he wiped the corner of my mouth with a napkin. Blushing, I scarfed the pancakes down.

"So I have the day off, what should we do?" Chase said, pulling my waist closer to his.

"Something different," I said, looking up at him hopefully. "You know this place better than I do, you choose."

"I think I might have an idea," Chase said, mysteriously. "Actually, go get ready now. We're leaving in half an hour."

"So spontaneous," I said. "I dig it."

I hurried off to the bathroom and took a quick shower. When I crossed into my bedroom, I noticed Chase was still in the kitchen, cooking God knows what.

"What should I wear?" I called down the hallway.

"Anything but formal!" Chase called back.

Well, that didn't help much. I settled on a jewel-toned tank top, a bold beaded necklace, white jean shorts, and silver gladiator sandals. I braided my wet hair and put on minimal makeup.

By the time I was ready, Chase had already cooked, packed the car, and managed to get dressed. It's remarkable how much time girls spend getting ready compared to guys.

"Now, there are a few rules. No questions, no comments, no concerns," Chase said, listing it off.

"Aw man, that means I cant speak!"

"I know, that's the point. Silence is golden," Chase said. "Don't worry, I have to follow the rules too. We both have to take the silence of the experience. It makes it more meaning-ful."

"Whatever you say," I shrugged. Ever since we were kids, Chase made up silly rules to the games we invented, thinking each rule had a specific purpose to exemplify the game experience.

Slipping on my sunglasses, I followed Chase to the car. He had put the Jeep Wrangler's top down, giving the car that con-vertible feel. As he speeded on the roads, the wind brushed against my face and hair. I closed my eyes, and savored the liberating yet relaxing experience.

Chase kept driving, driving, driving into the middle of nowhere. Eventually, he parked the car at a curb in the road, next to a large forest. Chase removed a picnic basket and blanket from the trunk of the car, and led me down a dirt path. Large, tangled, overcrowded trees surrounded us, casting peculiar shadows. The ground was soft and tamed by the wildlife, big boulders were covered with lush moss, and the trees were decked with large, hunter-green leaves. Birds chirped, squirrels scattered, and insects traveled in various directions. This was a brand new side of California that I had never seen before.

We kept walking, until we reached a peaceful stream. Chase laid the blanket out on the flat surface next to the stream. He pulled various sandwiches, salads, breads, pastries, dips, and all sorts of various foods. I had to fight off the urge to comment on his new exposed talent for cooking.

We divulged into our feast, taking in the scenery, enjoying each other's quiet company. Previously discovered, our relationship didn't need words or conversation. Being so well connected, we were able to communicate in other words – smiles, glances, body gestures – which made the experience much more powerful and enjoyable. Maybe Chase's rules weren't always ludicrous as I assumed.

Looking into Chase's eyes, I tried to say "thank you." His returned smile said "you're welcome." We packed up and strolled back to the car. I took in one last glance, knowing it was back to the beaches, sand, sunlight, and ocean waves.

We kept the silence going through the car ride, enjoying the passing sights as the sun began to set over them.

By the time we reached the house, it was dark. But not even darkness could conceal who was sitting on the front steps …

"Tyler," I whispered, pain aching in my heart. Chase's cheeks fumed with anger.

"What the fuck are you doing here?" Chase stormed up to Tyler. "How dare you show your face here, to us. After all the shit you've done. Get the fuck out of here, before I really lose it."

"Please, Chase, I came to apologize," Tyler said, vulnerability in his voice. Tyler looked pain stricken and exhausted, as if his guilt prevented him from sleeping last night.

"I don't want to hear your lame fucking apology," Chase said. "You know, Hayden's had enough apologies. From me, from Jessica, but not from you. You don't apologize, you don't admit your defeats, unless it's to benefit only yourself. I've had enough of your shit!"

I placed one hand on Chase's shoulder and the other on his chest, hoping to hold him off from Tyler.

I looked into Tyler's sad, tired and red eyes, then looked back at Chase. "Chase, please. Let him finish, and say what he needs to say. Please, for me."

CHAPTER 19

"Are you really going to tolerate his bullshit? That makes you almost as pathetic as he is," Chase scorned at me, his eyes red with fire, and his fists balling together.

"Hey," Tyler interfered. "Don't talk to her like that!"

Chase seemed to be taken back by this, by the way he instantly loosened his fists. His eyes narrowed down at me, the anger escaping from his pupils, as he said, "Ace, I'm so sorry, I didn't mean it."

"It's okay," I said, a little shaken by it. I just had to remind myself that this was Chase's way of coping about his father's illness. "I know you didn't mean it."

"Come on, we need to get you inside," I said, leading Chase into the house.

As I passed Tyler, I mouthed "I'm sorry." He nodded, acknowledging my sympathy.

His hands tangled behind his head, Chase stormed into the kitchen, trying to cool down. He slammed his fists down onto the counter and breathed heavily. Walking over, I tried to sooth him by rubbing him and wrapping my arms around his waist. Pressing my head into his back, I felt him inhale and exhale.

"I'm really sorry, Ace. I don't know what's going on with me lately! I just get so frustrated and angry, and I lose it, to the point where I don't even know who I'm attacking."

"I understand, Chase," I whispered, averting my gaze.

"I can tell your upset."

"I'm not. I was just frightened, but it's okay."

Chase tilted my chin so that I was forced to look at him. "Hayden, please, I don't want you to be afraid of me. I love you so much, and you have to know that I will never ever hurt you."

He kissed my forehead and pulled me into a tight embrace.

"But I don't want you to hurt Tyler either," I muttered into his chest. Biting my lip, I waited for his reaction. Chase loosened his grip around me, and took a step away from me.

"Why…do you keep sticking up for him? He's made nothing but trouble, and yet you keep giving him chances to make it up." I could hear the anger seeping back into his voice.

"I don't know," I stuttered. "I just feel like … he's not all bad. Just something is getting in the way, making him choose horrible decisions."

"And that one thing is his selfish motive to steal you away from me," Chase spat. "Can't you see? You're falling for his stupid little ploy. He's got you tied around a string, making you his little puppet. This is a classic-Tyler act. He's purposely making you feel bad, thinking maybe he's a good guy with a troubled life, when in reality he's just playing you, for his own entertainment. I can't believe, you of all people, would be completely blind to this. I thought you were different."

Chase stormed out of the kitchen, and slammed his bedroom door. When had we entered this parallel world, where everything was flipped? Where Tyler was being the good guy, while Chase was being the complete jerk?

Now, it was my turn to be angry.

I stomped over to his locked bedroom door, and banged on it. "You know what, Chase, you're wrong! You obviously don't have a soul, because if you did you would see that Tyler is sincere about everything. He's not putting on this act, so grow up and accept that people have more than one layer! And for the record, learn to control your temper, because I'm getting seriously fed up with your constant urge to fight."

When I finished screaming, I heard Chase turn up his stereo and blast some obnoxious music.

"Wow, aren't you cool! Blasting your music so you wont have to hear me. Real mature. Screw you Chase!"

Breathing heavily, I heaved over, feeling sick by everything that had happened. My body craved fresh air, so I struggled over to the front door. Taking one step outside instantly made me feel better. Not because of the oxygen filling my lungs, but because Tyler hadn't left.

Standing up, he faced me and shot me a puzzled look.

"Please, don't ask questions," I ordered. "Just take me away. Let's go somewhere."

Accepting my request, Tyler took me to his car. Similar to Chase's car, Tyler had a hunter-green Range Rover.

After buckling our seatbelts, Tyler asked, "Where do you want to go?"

"Anywhere, just away from here. You call the shots," I said, crossing my arms across my chest.

Knowing I wasn't in the mood for talking, Tyler turned up the music. I instantly recognized the song.

"You … like Billy Joel?" I asked, in utter surprise of his music choice.

"Are you kidding? I love him! I've got practically all of his albums."

"No way! I'm slightly obsessed with him!" I exclaimed. "You know, I never perceived you as a Billy fan."

"Element of surprise and deception," Tyler commented. "Most people don't know that I'm a classic rock junkie."

Winner, winner, chicken dinner. Someone had just seriously impressed me.

"I just gained so much respect for you," I said.

"Coming from you," Tyler said, taking his eyes from the road so he could look at me, "that means a lot. Thank you."

A modest smile rose on my face, and he returned it with a grin.

"Where are we headed, Pilot?"

"I'm not sure yet. I'm just kind of driving, wasting gas, but we'll find something," Tyler said. Laughing a little, I realized how much better I was feeling.

We kept driving, having a good time, blasting music, and losing track of time. Tonight was carefree. Where the two of us could run away from whatever problems we had, and just forget for a while. It was one of those times where we could say, "what the fuck, who cares!"

Finally, Tyler decided to park on the overhang of an abandoned road. Camping out on the hood of his car, we sat and admired the view of the light-filled town below us.

The cool air was getting to me, so Tyler draped his jacket around my shoulders.

"Thanks," I said, wrapping the jacket tighter around myself. "For everything you've done tonight."

Tyler's chocolate brown eyes looked into mine. "You're welcome, Hayden. I'm glad I could help."

"I guess I should tell you what happened now. I owe you that much." Tyler nodded for me to proceed. I explained what happened between Chase and I, giving him full detail and dialogue. When I finished, I realized how great it felt to have it off my chest.

"Thank you, for sticking up for me, but I'm really sorry that I got in the way. Look, I like you Hayden, but I would never personally go out of my way to destroy your relationship with Chase. I learned my lesson after the bet, but even when I kissed you, I had no intention of trying to steal you away. It just sort of happened, I couldn't help myself. And I felt horrible afterwards, so guilty and dirty. That's why I came to apologize, to both of you."

I put my finger up to his lips. "Tyler, I'm sick of apologies. I know, you don't need to say anything. And besides, what happened between Chase and me is not your fault. Our kiss is not the leading cause. I was the one who wanted to stick up for you, I was the one who wanted to give you more chances, and I was the one who wanted to protect you. Chase couldn't handle that, so he turned into a jerk."

Tyler looked at me, in awe of everything I had said. And yet, I didn't regret what I said, because it was all the truth. Yes, it could have been much easier to blame Tyler, but then I'd be a dishonorable bitch. Accepting the honest reality is simple, it's not always easy, but it's simple.

"You've probably heard this many times before, but you're different than other girls. There's just something about you . . ." Tyler said, his lips curling in curiosity.

I bit down on my bottom lip, and looked at him, with sparkling eyes. Hesitantly, Tyler inched his face towards mine.

"Kiss me," I whispered. "I want you to."

So he did. Surprisingly, I didn't feel guilty, not one bit. While I enjoyed kissing Tyler, I couldn't tell if I was doing it because I liked him, or I saw him as a rebound and a way to get revenge. But that was something to figure out later, for now it was "what the fuck, who cares!"

CHAPTER 20

"Look Hayden," Tyler said, breaking the kiss. "I can't do this, I'm sorry. As much as I want to keep kissing you, I know its wrong and I know you know its wrong too. I know that you really love Chase, a lot; by the way you look at him. And I know you're kissing me because you're confused, and you're not thinking clearly because of the fight."

I narrowed my eyes down. He was probably right; I was a little fazed by the fight.

"I'm sorry," was all I could say.

"It's okay," Tyler replied. "I should probably take you home now."

The car ride home was silent; no conversation, no music. Now that Tyler had pointed out my mistake, I felt guilty, dirty, and hypocritical. I had turned into my nightmare, my enemy.

What had I become? This unchill girl who doesn't under-stand and support her boyfriend who's going through a rough time? This bitchy slut who hooks up with another guy when she fights with her boyfriend?

Tyler pulled into the driveway and encouraged me to go find Chase and apologize. Maybe he wasn't as selfish as I thought he was.

Hanging my head low, I slugged into the house, preparing myself for a major break up.

Unlocking the front door, I noticed an envelope below my feet. I bent down and read it:

Letter 1 - May 2000

Deer Chase,

I hope you liek your new home! I miss u a lot! I want to see you soon! Right back soon.

Love, Hayden

Covering my mouth, I tried to keep myself from bursting into tears. I took a step into the house, and picked up the next letter.

Letter 2 - July 2000

Deer Chase,

I am glad to here everything is god! Summer is different without u! I miss my best frend!

Love, Hayden

This time I couldn't stop the tears. Chase had saved every single letter I sent to him when he moved to California. Taking another few steps, I picked up the next envelope.

Letter 3 - September 2000

Dear Chase,

Skool is very wierd without u! I am making new frends though! How is ur skool? Write back soon!

Love, Hayden

Tears of joy and tears of guilt. Chase was too good for me. I didn't deserve his sweet, adorable, romantic gesture. The next letter was place right in front of my closed bedroom door.

Letter 4 - December 2000

Dear Chase,

Today is my birthday! I wish you were hear to spend it with me! I miss you a lot! How are you? Come visit soon ok?

Love, Hayden

I opened my door, and found the last envelope strategically placed on my pillow.

Letter 5 - July 2010

Dear Hayden,

I'm incredibly sorry for what happened. I shouldn't have blown up at you like I did. It's your decision who you want to forgive, not mine, and I have to respect that. You have to believe me when I say I didn't mean what I said. I only said it because I panicked. But I don't want to panic anymore; I don't want to feel insecure about us. I trust you, Hayden. I promise I won't lose my temper at you anymore, and I'm going to try really hard to control my anger. Please, forgive me so we can make up?

Love, Chase.

PS - I love you so incredibly much.

By now, I was in full fledge tears. The guilt was overwhelming. Chase was blaming himself, but I was the true villain. He was so unaware of the damage I had done. Was this my punishment? Karma coming around and biting me in the ass? Giving me such an amazing, kind, incredible boyfriend to torture me because I was such a shitty and heartless girlfriend?

The sobs wouldn't stop; the whimpers were too loud to control.

"What's going on?" My mother bursted in, as a result of the loud noise I was making. "Baby, what's wrong?"

"Just go away, Mom! You wouldn't understand!"

"Hayden, I'm sorry," my mom said, sitting on the edge of my bed. "I'm all ears."

"Yeah now you are, but tomorrow you wont! Tomorrow you'll be out with Rebecca and John and Dad, taking care of either medical stuff or bonding with them! Well you know what, I'm sick of feeling neglected by you guys! And I know Chase is too! Did you guys ever think that maybe Chase needs his father most right now?"

My mother looked hurt. "We had no idea you guys felt that way. We thought you wanted to be left alone, parent free, and on your own."

"Well maybe you should think again," I said, regaining myself to some degree. My sadness about Chase had turned into anger about my parents. "I understand when your outings are cancer-related, but otherwise, I don't see why you guys can't set aside a day or two for Chase and I. Look, I don't want to talk anymore, I've got something else to do."

Before my mother could say anything else, I left my bedroom. Heading into John's office, I pulled out a piece of paper and an envelope. I began writing my heart away.

Letter 6 - July 2010

Dear Chase,

Please do not blame yourself. This wasn't your fault, it was mine. I reacted badly, and turned into something I'm not. After the fight, I lost it, and completely forgot what you were going through. I went outside, needing fresh air, and Tyler was sitting on the front steps. He hadn't left yet. So acting irrationally, I told him to take me away somewhere. So he did, and we drove to some random place. He listened to my problems, and then, I kissed him. I was just so angry and upset, and I wasn't thinking clearly. Soon after, Tyler helped me realize I only did it because I wanted my revenge on you, for making me feel so shitty. Words cannot describe the guilt I feel right now. I feel disgusting, vile, and cruel. When I got home, I saw all the letters you had saved from when we were kids. They all reminded me of how lucky I am to have such an amazing boyfriend. But then, how bitchy I am to go cheat on my amazing boyfriend. I understand if you want to break up, because I don't deserve a great guy like you. And I know that

I have to take the consequences of my actions. I just want you to know that I regret it entirely, because I really do love you. But in life, we make mistakes and we have to learn from them.

Love, Hayden.

Tears dropped onto the letter as I folded it up and slipped it into the envelope. As much as it hurt, I knew I was doing the right thing. Walking towards his bedroom, I slipped the letter under his door. Before leaving, I heard Rebecca calming speaking to Chase, apologizing for their absence. Thanks Mom, I thought.

Probably the hardest part about sending my explanation in a letterform was not getting an immediate reaction. I would have to wait until tomorrow morning to find out I had lost the greatest thing in my life. As hard as it was, I finally managed to fall asleep. It was weird sleeping in my own bed; not on the couch with Chase, not in Chase's bed. But I was going to have to get used to it, seeing as I had half a summer left without Chase.

"Hey Ace," Chase whispered. "Move over."

I was too asleep to realize what was happening under the circumstances. Rolling over onto my side, Chase slipped under the covers with me. He let me rest my head on his chest.

"So I got your letter," he whispered. Groggily nodding, I started to wake up slightly.

"Are you mad?" I asked.

"More just disappointed."

"Aw man, that's even worse!" I exclaimed, in a half asleep voice.

"Look, I'm willing to forgive but not forget. It's your turn to walk in my shoes. You're going to have to win my trust back, prove yourself, just like I had to. Prove that you love me, not Tyler. What kind of person would I be if you gave me a second chance, but I didn't give you one."

Tears started streaming down my cheek. "Thank you."

He lightly kissed my tear streaked face. "You're welcome. By the way, Rebecca knows about us. She said she wasn't very surprised."

I let out a light giggle, before falling asleep, tight in Chase's embrace.

CHAPTER 21

C hase's POV:

Honestly, I'm surprised at how well I reacted when Hayden told me. I guess it's because I feel somewhat responsible for what she did. Trying to cool off, I locked myself in my room and ignored Hayden, hoping she would understand. But she didn't, which makes me think maybe I could have handled the situation in a better way.

But hey, that's in the past and there's nothing I can do to change it now.

Waking up before Hayden, I delicately re-adjusted her sleeping position so that I could get up. Once I did, I took a shower, got dressed, and headed into the kitchen to start breakfast. My mother was pouring herself a cup of coffee.

When she saw me, she said, "Stacy and I are heading up to visit your father today. Do you think you and Hayden would like to tag along?"

"Um …" I pondered, unsure of my decision. I debated the two options before saying, "I don't think I'm ready for that quite yet."

Mom's eyes narrowed. "I understand, Baby. Just let me know when you are. It would mean a lot to your father."

"Soon," was all I managed to say, looking down at the ground. Rebecca nodded before leaving the kitchen.

What a shitty way to start off the day. My hands tingled with anger, but I fought the feeling off. I was going to keep my temper-controlling promise to Hayden.

After cooking for a good amount of time, I headed into Hayden's bedroom with a tray full of French Toast, Bacon and Orange Juice.

Placing the tray down, I gently woke her up.

"Breakfast in bed," I whispered, once her eyes were open. Pulling her knotty hair into a ponytail, she grinned at the sight of the food. Even with no makeup, messy hair, and bags under her eyes, I still thought Hayden was the most beautiful creature on this earth.

Hayden slid over, making room for me on the bed. Together, we shared the delicious meal I had cooked.

"So, I have to work today, but Rebecca says you are more than welcome to join her and visit John," I said, before sipping my juice.

"You didn't want to go?" Her voice sounded concerned.

I shook my head. "Not this time."

She paused, staring into my eyes. The thing about Hayden was that she knew me better than anyone. She could just take one look at me and know how I felt - as if she could read me like an open book.

"When you go, I'll go," Hayden said, taking my hand. Stroking her soft cheek, I kissed her forehead.

"I'll see you after work," I said, kissing her lips.

If I had it my way, I would spend every day with Hayden. Unfortunately, like every other teenager, I needed cash. Don't get me wrong, I loved my job - spending hours on the beach, hanging with some guy friends, getting a good salary - but time was running short, and I only had a month left with Hayden. The summer was flying by, and I needed more time with her. Three months together couldn't make up for the 10 years we were apart.

Strolling down to the shack, I prayed to be pair up with anyone other than Tyler. I didn't have enough stamina to deal with him, especially after what happened last night.

To my demise, the station board informed me that I was partnered with Tyler.

Bitterly, I stomped over to Chair 4. Tyler was already there, keeping guard, watching the crowd through his mirrored aviators. I pulled off my red Lifeguard shirt and climbed up the chair.

"Dude, I'm really sorry about last night," Tyler said, after I settled down.

"I'm sure you are," I said, sarcastically.

"Look, man, I am sorry. I shouldn't have come over to apologize, I shouldn't have taken Hayden out driving, and I shouldn't have kissed her! But we all make mistakes!"

"What you did was more than a mistake. It was a choice between right and wrong, good and bad. And making a shitty decision is your fault."

Tyler sat silent for a moment, soaking in my harsh words. "Just because you're going through a rough time doesn't give you the right to be a full-on jerk. Be mad, be angry, do whatever you need to, but be aware that you're hurting the people you love. Last night, you really hurt Hayden. And for the past few weeks, you've been hurting me."

"Whatever."

"Good answer. No really, excellent fucking response. It's really nice to see that my best friend actually cares," he spat, sardonically. Anger was fuming in his cheeks.

Best friend, his voice rang in my head. In the past few weeks, I had forgotten the fact that we were such good friends. All the anger, fighting, and backstabbing had concealed the real depth of our friendship.

"Tyler . . . I do care," I said, suddenly aware of the damage I had done.

"Yeah? Well you have a really shitty way of showing that you do. Seriously, I don't believe you for a second. The only person you care about is Hayden. Everyone else doesn't matter because they're too flawed for your taste. I make bad decisions, so you feel the need to attack me. Jessica broke your trust, so you automatically stop talking to her. Newsflash! You're not perfect! And neither is Hayden! She ran off with me, she kissed me, she cheated on you! So wake up and stop pretending like you two are so much better than the rest of us."

"You asshole …" I gritted, my hands twisting into fists. "How dare you say that about her. Take that back."

Climbing down the steps, Tyler said, "Make me."

I was just about to follow him down and give him a piece of my mind, when I remembered two things that stopped me.

1. My promise to Hayden

2. If the chair was left empty during watch hours, I would lose my job.

So while Tyler managed to escape my wrath, I was left stranded on the chair, to sulk in my frustration.

Hayden's POV:

After Chase left, I called Carmen up for some major brainstorming. Operation "Win Trust Back" was in motion.

When she arrived, I blasted into a full detailed summary of the night. By the end, Carmen's mouth was dropped in awe.

"What is it with Tyler? He's just full of unexpected surprises," Carmen said, almost with a pleased toned.

"Tell me about it …"

"Maybe he's not such a bad guy," Carmen shrugged, with a sparkle in her eye. "He did come to apologize, and he even helped you come to your senses."

"Well yeah. He's a great guy, with a tough exterior, but he's no Chase."

"No he's definitely not." Carmen tied her hair up in a ponytail, preparing for work mode. "Okay time for the game plan. You need to prove to Chase that Tyler means nothing to you."

"Yes, I do."

"Okay, as of now, I only see one solution," she said. I nodded for her to go on. "You need to cut off all connection with Tyler. Not forever, just until Chase sees that you're willing to commit to only him."

"Yeah, that what I was thinking too, but does that mean I can't even be friends with him?"

Carmen shook her head. "For the time being, no."

"But if I can't be friends with him, how will I be able to play match maker and set you two up?"

Carmen playfully shoved me and exclaimed, "How did you know?"

"Oh please, you're not very good at hiding it," I said, raising an eyebrow at her. "I will admit though, I didn't notice until today. How long have you liked him?"

"Since I started working at the Sandy Shell. He's so sweet, cute, and he's got that badass attitude that I absolutely love.

But I've always thought he was a total player. But after what you told me, I see that my perception was wrong."

Grinning with delight, I realized that everything was working out pretty well.

"But wait, were you jealous at all?"

"Maybe just a little, because I wanted that to be me … but I never worried too much about the two of you, because I knew you would always choose Chase over Tyler."

I pulled her into a tight embrace, and we both squealed a little in excitement.

"Okay, okay," Carmen said, post phoning the excitement. "One thing at a time! My shift starts soon, so why don't come with me to work and talk to Tyler there?"

"Yeah perfect," I said. I grabbed a sticky note and wrote a quick message to Chase, letting him know I would be back soon.

During the car ride, I tried not to over think what I would say to Tyler. This wasn't going to be the most delightful conversation, but it had to be done.

Once we got to the Pier, the nerves started kicking in. My stomach knotted in uneasiness. Even though I knew it was for the better, I still wished that there was some other alternative. But I needed to save my relationship with Chase, I needed his trust back, and this was the only way.

CHAPTER 22

S tanding in front of the restaurant, I took a deep breath, trying to suppress my nausea

"It's going to be fine, he'll understand," Carmen said, trying to comfort me. "Take your time."

Watching her head into the restaurant, I tried to reassure myself a few more times. When I was somewhat ready, I scrambled in and searched for Tyler. Sitting at his regular stool at the bar, he hung over his drink, tracing the rim with his fingers.

"Hey," I said, sliding onto the stool next to him.

"Hey," he said, slightly surprised to see me. "How . . . um are you?"

"I'm better," I said, reviewing my unstable mentality of last night. "How are you doing?"

"Not so well. Since last night, I've felt incredibly guilty. And today's fight with Chase didn't help much either," he said, staring into his glass.

"Yeah, I'm really sorry about that...and everything. It was my fault, and you shouldn't take the blame for any of it. Actually, I should thank you, because you were the one who stopped it, and helped me realize what I was doing was wrong."

"Well, I'm glad I could help," he said, with a gloomy melancholy tone.

"Tyler, you're a great guy, but unfortunately I don't think we can be friends," I whispered, my voice quivering. "Believe me, I want to be, but after last night, Chase doesn't trust me. The only way I can imagine earning his trust back is by ending all connections with you . . . at least for the time being, until things blow over."

Tyler looked up from his glass, and widens his eyes at me, in utter shock.

"That's the only way?"

Nodding, I bit down on my lip and tried to fight the tears that were welling in my eyes.

"I'm sorry it has to come to this, because I really like being friends with you, but I see no other options, and I can't bear to lose Chase."

Tyler paused before saying, "I understand."

Those two words were enough for me to lose it. "Are you mad? Please don't be mad! God, I hate this! Because I do care about you - just not in the romantic way. And I wish I could have it both ways; I could keep Chase as my boyfriend and keep you as my guy friend! But I can't, so I feel like I'm bearing torn into two parts, being forced to choose!"

By this point, the tears had overcome my attempts and started streaming down my face. Why this made my so emotional, I'll never know, but something told me that this situation meant something to me. Just because I wasn't interested Tyler, didn't mean he wasn't important in my life.

"Hey, hey," Tyler said, jumping up from his seat. He pulled me up to my feet and clasped my hands. "You don't have to choose."

"I don't?" I looked up at him, puzzled.

He wiped my tear-stained cheek. "No, this may be the only option, but there are ways around it. Like, we could keep our friendship a secret."

Taking a few minutes, I considered this. If we kept our friendship on the down low, I could lie to Chase and say I cut off all connection with Tyler.

"No way . . . no, no," I shook my head, suddenly rejecting the idea. "I couldn't do that to Chase. I can't lie or betray him again."

"Okay, okay, I know. It was just a thought."

"I know, it was a good suggestion," I replied. "But I don't think I could ever do that. It wouldn't be right . . . hey, aren't you the guy whose supposed to help me do the right thing?"

"Well yeah," Tyler said, letting out a small chuckle. "That was one time. Remember, I'm not exactly the face of good decision making."

"Why not make it a second time? A third time! You're a good guy Tyler, just a little misguided." Seeing how well the upbeat the conversation was turning out to be, I decided to take it in a new direction. "I think so, and so does Carmen?"

His eyes sparkled a little. "She does? What did she say?"

"Something along those lines. I'd say she's actually pretty interested in you," I said, toying with him a little bit.

"Really? How do you know? I kind of got that vibe from her, but I also got the vibe that she thought I was a player."

"Well, you are a player. And she did think that, but she knows that when you want to be, you're a really sweet and caring guy."

"Well, if I don't have a chance with you, I might as well give it a shot with her," Tyler shrugged. "Maybe she's the key to getting over you."

Smiling at his openness, I said, "Absolutely brilliant. And you know, if you're not a threat anymore, Chase will most likely let us be friends."

"I really hope so," Tyler said, revealing a smile.

Now that things were settled between us, I headed home. It's kind of bizarre how problems always solve themselves. Things just always end up working out, which was a reassuring and comforting fact of life.

Walking through the front door, I hear The Vampire Diaries playing from the living room. Leaving the door open and tip toeing over, I leaned over the back of the couch, and surprised Chase with an upside down kiss, Spiderman style.

"Hey beautiful," he said, lifting his head up to look at me. Rotating, I slipped my arms around his neck and flopped down on top of him. "What put you in such a good mood?"

"I have the best news," I said, giddy. "I think you'll be really happy to hear it."

"Go on," he said, with an eager smile.

"I just got back from the Sandy Shell. And . . . I just broke off all connection with Tyler. I told him straight up that we couldn't be friends anymore."

"You did that . . . for me?" Chase said, with his eyebrows raised.

Nodding, I said, "Yes, in hopes to prove my love and loyalty."

Chase tilted my chin and kissed me gently and tenderly. "Just because you were willing to sacrifice a friendship for me, indicates that I can trust you again."

A huge smile spread across my face, and I gave him a huge kiss. "Thank you!"

"No, thank you," Chase said, between the kisses. I wrapped my arms tighter around his neck, and he held onto my waist.

After we finished making out, I said, "Even though it was only one day without your trust, it was the longest day of my life! I have no idea how you lasted a whole week!"

"Neither do I!" Shrugging, Chase smiled a big white grin. His blue eyes sparkled at me as he said, "So shall we continue the Vamp D's marathon?"

"Vamp D's?" I snorted. "Cute nickname."

"Isn't it? I'm hoping if I say it enough, it will catch on. All phrases start out small," Chase remarked, jokingly.

"Good luck with that," I teased, playfully smiling.

After a few episodes, we felt a sharp jolt. Suddenly, everything in the house started uncontrollably shaking. Alert, Chase and I jumped up.

Rebecca, my mother and father ran inside from the porch. "GET OUT FAST! EARTH QUAKE."

Running, we all exited the front door.

"Let's all take my car," Rebecca instructed.

"Where are we going?" I asked, feeling completely out of the loop.

"Shelter," Rebecca informed.

"Why do we have to go? Can't we just stay outside until the earth quake is over?"

Everyone headed towards the car, so I followed, hoping someone would eventually answer my question. Awkwardly, my father joined Chase and I in the back seat.

"We're in a really badly affected area. There's a good chance that the foundation might be destructed, so it's not safe. And sometimes, after the big earthquake, smaller eruptions tend to follow. It's just much safer if we spend the night at the shelter," Chase explained. Of course, being the Connecticuter, I was blissfully unaware of the dangers of earthquakes.

To my surprise, much of the town was at the shelter. Rebecca told us we could go wander around, meet up with friends and perhaps share a room with them.

To our luck, we quickly found Tyler and Carmen, who were huddled together, flirting and chatting away.

"Oh," I whispered, as we approached them. "I forgot to tell you, Carmen is into Tyler . . . and from the looks of it, Tyler is into her."

Chase stopped in his tracks. "Does this mean he doesn't like you anymore?"

"I guess not," I said, shrugging.

"I think I owe someone an apology," Chase muttered. My lips curled into a small smile, even though I pretended as if I didn't hear him.

"Hey guys," I said, greeting the two of them. Startled from their lovey-dovey la la land, they bolted up.

"What's up?" Chase said, clasping Tyler's hand in a very bro way. "Can we talk for a bit?"

Before breaking into a massive conversation, Carmen and I waited for the boys to be out of hearing distance. When they were, we squealed in excitement.

"Tell me everything!" I demanded. Carmen gestured for me to sit on the plastic blue chair up against the bland, white, concrete wall.

"Okay, so after you left, Tyler came up to me. We started talking and he admitted how he always liked my edge style and personality. I told him how I always thought his bad ass appeal was really sexy and we just hit it off. We're going out tomorrow night!"

Pulling her into a bouncing embrace, we celebrated the good outcome. Things were flawlessly falling into place. At this rate, everything would be solved in no time.

CHAPTER 23

C hase and Tyler came back, laughing. Wrapping his arm around her shoulders, Tyler led Carmen down the hallway.

"So I apologized to Tyler for acting so irrationally, and he totally understood, so we're all better," Chase said, smiling with satisfaction.

"That's great!"

"Yeah, I'm really happy. And he said we are more than welcome to spend the night with them," Chase said. "They've already got a room and everything."

"Won't that be . . . awkward?"

Chase cocked his head to the side, puzzled by my words.

"Because . . . I told Tyler I couldn't be friends with him anymore," I explained, sullenly.

"Oh that? Just because you were even willing to do that for me, shows that I can trust you," Chase said, stroking my jaw line. "If you were able to cut off all connection with him, that must mean you have no feelings for him. Besides, Tyler seems into Carmen, so I'm not worried about him trying to steal you away."

"So, does that mean I can be friends with him again?" I asked, trying to swallow my excitement.

"Of course," Chase said, twisting his fingers in my jean belt loops, pulling me closer to him. "You know, I would have never actually made you end your friendship with him, but I'm glad you did it on your own, because it shows me you were willing to do anything to win my trust back."

Gazing into his eyes, I stood on my tip toes so that my lips reached his. Delicately, our lips touched, sending an electric shock through my body.

"Come on," Chase whispered, breaking the kiss. "We should probably tell our parents where we will be for the night."

Slipping our arms around each other, we searched for our parents. We found them, huddled in a corner. My parents were chatting about the earthquake, while Rebecca was on the phone. I shot my mother a puzzled look.

"John," she mouthed. From that, I tuned into Rebecca's side of the conversation.

"Well, I'm glad to hear everything is okay over there . . . no, we're not sure how much damage is done, but I'm sure insurance will cover it . . . uh huh . . . okay, I'll call them . . . yeah we're all fine, the kids are here too . . . yeah one sec . . ."

Rebecca took the phone off her ear, and covered the mouth piece with her hand. "Chase, he's asking for you."

With a deep breath, Chase took the phone. When he heard John's voice, his eyes instantly brightened. Wandering as he talked, Chase broke into full conversation.

"I'm glad to see Chase is willing to talk," Rebecca commented. "I just hope he'll want to visit John soon."

"Baby steps," my mother cooed. She was right; Chase just needed some time, and eventually he'd build up to it. Yet, time was running out, and nobody could predict when it was too late.

Time can be both positive and detrimental. Sometimes, time is the best remedy to any situation. But sometimes, time is of the essence, and if you lose track of it, it bites you in the ass.

Thinking of this, I realized that the sand in the summer hour glass was draining fast. It was already late July, and time was flying by. Chase and I haven't even discussed what was going to happen once the summer ended.

Chase came back, with a huge smile on his face.

"Your turn," he said, extending his hand that held the cell phone.

"Hey Uncle John."

"Hey kiddo," he spoke, in a scratchy, weak voice. "Holding down the fort for me?"

"Of course, you can count on me."

"Glad to hear the positive report," he said, chuckling. The projection of his laugh sounded as if it caused him pain. "So Chase gave me the full update on you too."

Blushing slightly, I was thankful he couldn't see me. "Oh yeah?"

"Yeah. Take care of him for me, okay? Make sure he doesn't do anything stupid."

Flattered by the fact that John trusted and relied on me for a favor, I said, "Will do, Uncle John. I'll keep an eye on him."

"Thanks kiddo," he said. "Well, make sure to visit soon and I'll talk to you in a few days!"

"Bye Uncle John!" Reaching over, I handed Rebecca the phone. She said her goodbyes, she hung up and snapped the phone closed.

"So where are you kids going to be tonight?" Rebecca asked, cheerfully

Chase gave the details, including the room number, in case they needed to find us. We said our goodnights, and were sent on our way.

"John sounds good," I said, as we started strolling through shelter.

"Yeah, he does," Chase muttered.

"You seemed pretty happy afterwards," I commented.

"Yeah, it was good finally talking to him," Chase admitted. "We talked, caught up, and I realized how much I miss him."

Thinking of Rebecca's concern, I said, "Do you think you'll want to visit him soon?"

"Perhaps," he said, with a slight smile. "If I'm feeling up to it, I will."

The room door was wide open, and we found Carmen and Tyler involved in an aggressive game of Rummy 500. They were sitting on a bland, white-sheeted bed, facing each other. Another plain bed was on the other side of the room.

"Can we get in on this fun?" Chase said, interrupting their game flow.

Carmen giggled, and gathered the cards together. "Come closer and join us, we don't bite."

Chase pushed the empty bed towards the center of the room, so we were closer the other couple. Tyler got up and placed a cheap, wooden bedside table between both beds. Carmen shuffled the deck, dealt four hands of 7 cards, put the rest of the deck in the center, face down. Taking the top card of the deck, she flipped it face up and placed it next to the stack.

"The game is simple. We rotate left of the dealer, and when it's your turn you can either draw the top card from the stack and keep it, or pick up as many cards from the discard pile," she said, pointing to the flipped face card. "To get points, you must place down three of a kind, or a straight. At the end of your turn, you must get rid of one card and add it to the discard pile. We play till everyone runs out of cards, then add up the score points."

As the game went on, our competitive sides came out. We laughed, we screamed, we sang, we swore, but most of all, we had a good time. For the first time, all four of us were able to have a carefree, quality, bonding experience. All the drama, fights, and tension was forgotten and in the past. It felt like nothing, nobody could ruin this . . .

Except for Jessica.

Carelessly, we had left our door wide open, allowing anybody to peer in. Poor, lonely Jessica must have been strolling around the shelter alone.

Knocking on the open door, she said, "Hey guys."

Our laughter, fun, and game stopped, as we all turned up to look at her. Silence and awkwardness filled the room. While Jessica was not completely hated among us, she was not exactly loved. As Chase's bitchy ex girlfriend and Carmen's long time rival, Jessica was only on good terms with Tyler and me.

"Hey Jess," I said, forcing a warm and friendly tone. "How's it going?"

"Good, minus the earthquake," she replied. Each of us forced an awkward chuckle. "Can I join?"

"Well, we're kind of already in the middle of a game," Carmen sneered. "So you're going to have to wait till we finish."

I glared at Carmen, for her rudeness and contradiction. Earlier, Carmen had cut her game short with Tyler to include Chase and me.

"Th-that's okay," Jessica stuttered, obviously hurt by the words. "I don't mind."

Awkwardly, Jessica grabbed a plastic chair from the hallway and dragged it into the room, next to the table. She sat uncomfortably between the two couples. Occasionally sneaking a glance at her, I noticed that she looked upset, like she was trying to force back some tears. It was clear that Jessica knew she wasn't accepted.

We all tried getting back into the game, but it wasn't the same. The energy and flow could not be re-created. But we pushed on, and finally finished the game. Carmen, being the card expert, won. Chase came in second, I third, and Tyler last. Carmen playfully teased him and told him to never go to Vegas.

"Should we start another game?" Tyler asked, hoping to redeem himself as well as considering Jessica. Jessica's body language instantly relaxed, knowing her discomforted wait was over.

Faking a yawn, Carmen said, "I'm actually pretty tired. Let's call it quits for the night."

Even though I wasn't the one being unfairly treated, my body was boiling with anger. Just because Carmen doesn't favor Jessica, doesn't give her the right to be an outward, rude bitch!

"Okay," Jessica's voice quivered. "I guess I'll just see you guys later."

Picking up speed, Jessica quickly exited the room.

"Now look what you've done," I scorned Carmen, before running after Jessica. Yes, Jessica wasn't the nicest girl in the world, but nobody deserves to be treated like crap.

"Jessica," I called down the hallway. "Wait up!"

Jogging down the squeaky hallway, I caught up to Jessica, who was already in full-on tears.

"I'm so sorry about Carmen. You didn't deserve that sort of treatment, and Carmen should know that."

Jessica said something, but her sobs made it completely indistinguishable. People roaming through the shelter were beginning to stare, so I hurried her off to the closest bathroom. Turning on the sink, she rinsed her face to cool off - total déjà vu.

When she was all better, she said, "I just can't believe it. Lately, I'm trying so hard to be nice and friendly, but nothing seems to work. Even when I'm doing my best at being a good person, I'm still labeled and treated as a bitch. What's the point anymore! Nobody likes me anymore! Not girls, not guys, nobody!"

"Don't say that, Jessica," I said, firmly. "Don't even think that, because it's not true. You have tons of other friends! Carmen and you have always had difficulties, tonight it was just magnified. And things will always be awkward with Chase, as it is with every ex. Don't let one sour night with one sour girl get you down. Don't let it stop you from trying your hardest to be a good person, because eventually it will pay off. It just takes a little effort and determination, but it's worth the work."

"I'm just so sick of everyone still treating me like the bad guy," Jessica muttered, wiping a tear away.

"It sucks, but years of bad attitude doesn't erase overnight," I said, trying to be honest yet sympathetic. "But it will get better, I promise."

"You sure?" Jessica looked at me, wide eyed. I nodded, and gave her a slight smile. "Alright, we'll I probably should get back. Thanks, Hayden."

"No problem, I'm always here."

Leaving the bathroom, we headed in different directions. Running my hand across my face, I prepared myself to confront Carmen.

CHAPTER 24

W alking into the room, I didn't have an idea where to even begin. Raging with anger, Carmen marched up to me.

"Why would you go after her like that? I thought you were on my side," she sneered.

I put my hands up, defensively. "Whoa, when did this turn into World War III, with the allies and axis?"

"That's not the point. You're my best friend . . . you're supposed to support me."

"So, I'm supposed to support my best friend, even when she's being an inconsiderate, cold-hearted bitch? I don't know about you, but that doesn't sound right to me," I said, with a dose of sarcasm.

"I'm not the bitch," she growled. "She is!"

"Actually you're wrong, Carmen. You see, Jessica has been trying her hardest to be a better person. And if I recall, she hasn't personally victimized in quite a while," I replied.

"Well she did something to you," Carmen muttered. "And when someone hurts my friend, it's almost like hurting me."

While in theory Carmen was being a good friend, there is a fine line, one that she crossed. You can support, side and remain loyal to a friend, but only to a certain extend. If this had happened a few weeks ago, before Jessica had apologized, then Carmen would be justified. However, present day, that was not the case.

"I know you had good intentions, but things have been put in the past. Things have changed, and people like Jessica are trying to change. Holding grudges, for personal or outside reasons, is never a good way to live in the present and future."

Dolefully, Carmen stared at the ground, and meekly said, "I probably should go apologize."

Giving her a pat on the shoulder, I sent her off to take responsibility of her actions.

After she left, Tyler said, "Well today has just been full of surprises."

"You can say that again," I muttered, collapsing onto the bed in exhaustion Chase sat beside me, stroking my hair.

"You did the right thing," Chase whispered in my ear. "It was really noble of you to calm Jessica down when nobody else wanted to."

My response was a mere shrug. Desperately, I needed a hug. Completely forgetting that we weren't alone, I wrapped my arms around Chase. He provided me with that same, old, safe and secure feeling.

Uncomfortably, Tyler cleared his voice, reminding us of his presence. Chase and I broke the embrace, and we all exchanged glances. There was denying the air of awkwardness. Without Carmen, the three of thrown back into the mess we were in a few days ago; Tyler on the outs of my relationship with Chase.

As happy as I was for the new couple, I doubted the legitimacy of their feelings. Just days before, Tyler was fawning over me. Just hours before, Carmen was convinced Tyler was a full-on player with no heart. I felt as though the two of them were moving quickly, as their emotions struggled to keep speed.

But who was I to judge their relationship? All that matter was they were happy together, right?

"I think I'm going to go find Carmen," Tyler said, obviously uncomfortable with being the third wheel. Not surprised, I watched him exit the room and head down the hallway.

After he left, Chase said, "So, how do you think things are going?"

"I don't know," I replied. Leaning back, I felt myself flopped back onto the bed, resting my head on the unfamiliar pillow. "Pretty good, I guess."

"He still likes you," Chase muttered.

"I figured," I said, flipping onto my side. "It's just a transition. He'll get over it soon."

"Yeah, I hope so," Chase said, stroking my leg.

Exhausted from the long, action filled day, we decided to turn in for the night. Without Tyler and Carmen, we turned off the lights and snuggled under the shelter provided covers. Chase, sleeping on the left side of the bed, placed his arm around my waist.

"Goodnight, Ace," he whispered. "I love you."

"I love you too," I replied, softly kissing him.

By the time I woke up the next morning, everyone was already up and moving, packing up to leave. Rounding my spare belongings together, I caught pace with everyone. Chase informed me that we were going back to house, despite the damages done.

The car ride home was silent, as we all anticipated the degree of destruction. As we passed the community, we saw structures in shambles, electric poles and trees shattered, and streets filled with debris. The sights only foreshadowed the appearance of the Levine's beach house.

With a smashed pillar, the house was left with a tilted foundation. Branches had fallen onto the roof, dislodging a number of shingles. As well as a few windows had been cracked. I gasped at the devastating sight.

"The inside is always worst," Chase muttered, fazed by the damage. All at once, we entered through the tattered front door, hoping for some relief.

Chase was right. Rebecca's blue and white designed China plates that were once on display were now laying in pieces on the floor. The television in the living room was broken and dented.

"I guess we'll have to put off the Vamp D's off for a while," Chase said, running his hand over the cracked screen. Before we searched the rest of the house, I placed a comforting hand on his shoulder.

We checked the bedrooms next. At first glance, I was overwhelmed by the condition of my room. Things had been thrown off, piled together, and cluttered in sections. The quaint Coastline portraits had fallen down while the white wicker dresser had keened over. Chase helped me lift it back into place, and luckily it was still intact, with just a few scratches. Checking my guitar, I was thankful I had put it in it's safe, protecting case.

"How's it look in your room?" I asked, after he helped me tidy up a bit.

"Nothing too severe, just my stereo will need some repairs," he shrugged off. As a resident of California, he definitely knew the difference between a little and a lot of damage caused by earthquakes.

We met up in John's study, where our parents were cleaning up. His large, oak desk had a huge crack down the middle. His fully loaded bookshelves had tipped over, scattering classic novels all around. Picking up The Great Gatsby, I handed the thick covered novel over to Rebecca, who was trying to organize the books.

"Thanks sweetie," she said, putting in a specific pile. "Why don't you two go out for a bit, and let us take over. You guys shouldn't be inside cleaning on such a beautiful day as this."

That was like the comments Rebecca used to use when were kids. She would always try to get us outside, in the sunshine. If were playing cards on the kitchen table, she would tell us we could bring the card deck out onto the porch and play there. If we were drawing, she told us to bring our coloring books out to the lawn.

"You could use the help, Mom. The more hands, the faster," Chase said.

"With just the adults combined, we've got six hands," Rebecca retorted. "That's the same number we usually have. Go out and have fun."

Obeying her orders, we got changed into our bathing suits, and headed for the beach. Most people were taking care of their homes, which left the beaches practically deserted.

"Got any ideas?" I said, kicking my bare feet through the sand.

"I wonder if their open . . ." Chase pondered, asking himself.

"Who?"

"You'll see," he said, heading towards the south side of the beach. "Let's go."

After a distance of walking, we reached a lone beach shack, badly affected by the earthquake. The faded Willy's Beach Equipment sign was deep in the sand.

Watching his step as he entered the tattered doorway, Chase said, "Will, you in here?"

Two men - one on the large, pudgy side and the other tan and toned – were cleaning up broken wood and metal pieces.

"Bro, how's it going?" The tan one greeted us, while the pudgy one lingered in the back as he continued to clean.

"As good as it usually goes after a quake. How'd you make out, Will?" Chase asked, sneaking a glance of the mess.

Will shrugged. "Seen worse. Now, whose this unfamiliar lady?"

"I'm Hayden," I said, feeling slightly out of place.

"Wicked. It's cool to meet you," he said, flipping his uncut hair.

"You wouldn't happen to have any Jet Skis in good condition?" Chase asked.

Instantly, I widened my eyes. What was he thinking? If I couldn't handle a surfboard, then I sure as hell couldn't handle an entire, motorized jet ski!

"Usually, I wouldn't do business right now, considering the state of the shop, but for you, I'll make an exception," Will said, patting Chase on the shoulder. Heading towards the back of the shack, he called, "How many do you need? Two?"

Jabbing Chase, I loudly whispered, "Are you crazy? You saw me after the surf accident! Are you trying to get me killed?"

"Precisely," Chase said, with an eye roll. "Yeah, two will work."

Will clanked around, as he rummaged around in the mess. Before we knew it, two very shiny, blue and white Jet Skis were before us. Their top appearance looked out of place in the cluttered, destroyed shack.

"How much do I owe you?" Chase said, pulling his wallet out of his swim truck pocket.

"Free of charge, bro. Pay me back by letting me know when the next big boat party is," Will said, nudging Chase.

"You'll be the first to know," Chase said. They exchanged a tight, guy-styled, handshake.

"Come on, I'll set you guys up."

With remarkable strength, Will moved the skis out to the edge of the shore. He gave me a tutorial, instructing all the gadgets and buttons.

"Do you know how many people die from Jet Ski accidents per year?" I asked nervously, snapping the clasp on my life jacket.

He let out a deep, goofy laugh. "You wont die."

"You'd be surprise of what I'm capable of," I muttered.

Chase started up his engine. "You ready, Ace?"

"Nope. If I get hurt, I'm blaming you." Hesitantly, I turned the water proof key, which sent a roar of vibration through the water vehicle.

"And I'm okay with that!" Chase shouted over the noise, before skidding into the crashing water.

Chase made it look easy, but unfortunately, he was much more coordinated than me. Nevertheless, with a twist of the handle, I drove into the water. My logic was if kept a steady and slow speed, I could remain alive.

While my ride was rather calming and enjoyable, Chase rode like a wild child, which looked much more exhilarating. He managed to travel in circles around me, as I cruised up and down the shore line.

At one point, he slowed down and rode silently beside me. But not for long, because he ended up revving up his engine, challenging me to a race.

"NO!" I shouted, over the sound of the loud motors and crashing waves.

"YOU KNOW YOU WANT TO."

He knew me too well. One tiny, little race couldn't hurt, right? As long as I managed to stay focused and controlled.

My lips curled into a devilish, wild child smile. Before any countdown, I gave my ski a jolt of gas. Rapidly gaining speed, I felt recklessness and adrenaline power me. As my hair whipped through the wind, mists and spray coated my face. I felt weightless and free, as if I was flying over the cool, crisp seawater.

One glance behind me was all I needed to lose balance. As I sneaked a peek to see where Chase was, I felt my body kilter off the vehicle, into the water. My clumsiness didn't surprise me, but my ability to float to the top of the surface, unharmed and laughing, did. Thank you, life jacket.

Chase speeded over next to me, and cut the engine on both of our skis.

"Are you okay? Are you hurt? What happened?"

Uncontrollably laughing, I floated on my back and kicked the water with my legs. The thrill of falling was almost as good as the rush of energy I got from the ride.

"Again, again!" I cheered like a five year old. Hoisting myself up, I regained my position on the Jet ski. With a quick wrist movement, I started the engine and drove off.

Forgetting the little incident, we continued to race. After a while I got the hang of it, and was able to ride comfortably without precautions.

Chase led us out to an abandoned island, secluded and empty. Having the land to ourselves, we spent the majority of our time making out. Kissing him, knowing he was all mine and I was all his, was the best feeling in the world. We no longer worried about Jessica's revenge or Tyler's ploy of feelings. For once, our relationship was a two way street, not four way intersection.

CHAPTER 25

Unfortunately, we had to leave our peaceful paradise and return the jet skis. However, escaping from the world, if only for a few hours, with the person I love was absolutely priceless.

After the jet skis were under Willy's possessions, we strolled back to the house. The transformation was astonishing – so remarkable that I actually thought my eyes were playing a trick on me. Aside from the off balanced level of the foundation, everything was organized and refurbished. Broken furniture was removed, and every undamaged item was back in its proper place.

"See," Rebecca said when she saw us, as she swept the kitchen floor. "We could do it without you guys. All you needs is some elbow grease and determination."

"I'm very impressed," Chase said, kissing his mother on the cheek.

"Tomorrow, we shop till we drop!" Rebecca exclaimed, obviously excited at the idea of new, state of the art items replacing the old, out-dated, broken furniture.

"Actually, I was thinking we could go visit Dad tomorrow," Chase said, earnestly.

Rebecca and I raised our eyebrows in utter shock. "Really?"

"Well yeah, after talking to him last night, I realized that I really want to see him," Chase explained. "I'm ready."

"Okay, I'm sure we can schedule a visit," Rebecca said, trying her best to hide the huge smile that was located on her beaming face.

"Great," he said, heading down the hallway.

When his back was turned, the two of us instantly made eye connection. Rebecca no longer forced her smile away, as it contagiously spread onto me.

"Can you believe it?" She whispered.

"I know," I whispered back, through a toothy grin. Relief and pride washed over me – Chase was finally ready to put on his big-boy pants and face the ugly truth.

"John's going to be so happy to finally see him," Rebecca said, a little louder than a whisper.

"I leave the room for one minute, and I come back to find you two talking about me," Chase remarked, on the joking side. Tucked under his arm was a beach towel, and in his right hand was the picnic basket we used on the last date.

"Sorry," we both muttered in unison.

I watched Chase rummaged through the kitchen, as he selected a variety of dining essentials – plates, utensils, and glasses. After whispering in Chase's ear, Rebecca winked at me and exited the room.

"Why don't you get dressed into something warmer?" Chase suggested. I raised a suspicious eyebrow at him, but followed his advice.

In my bedroom, I traded in my damp bathing suit for warm cotton undergarments. I put on some black yoga pants and pulled a warm, fuzzy sweatshirt over my head. After brushing my salty hair, I twisted it into a loose braid.

"Ready Freddie?" Chase asked when I re-entered the kitchen.

"Sure thing," I shrugged.

Taking our usual route - out the back door, through the porch, down the stairs – we found a comfortable spot on the shore, with a perfect view of the sunset. Spreading the towel out across the cool sand, we sat down. Chase piled some salad onto a china plate, and handed it to me.

"Turkey or ham?" He asked, offering me a choice of sandwich.

"Turkey!"

Pulling out two saran wrapped sandwiches, he handed the T sharpie labeled one to me. After unveiling the ham sandwich, he took a hearty bite and positioned it on his plate.

Reaching into the picnic basket again, he pulled out two clear, plastic wine glasses and a bottle of white wine.

"Courtesy of Rebecca," he said, extending the bottle in my view so I could read the label: Monthaven Winery Chardonnay 2007.

So that was the secret Rebecca exchanged with Chase when we were in the kitchen.

"As appealing as it sounds," I started. "I don't think I should. You remember the last time I drank. No thank you, I don't want to head down that road ever again."

Against my wishes, he started pouring me a glass. "That's because it was your first time drinking. It always hits you the hardest the first time, and especially if you don't know how to control yourself."

After pouring into both glasses, he handed one to me. Hesitantly, I took a sip, letting the green grape flavor fill my throat. Unlike last time, I could barely taste the alcohol.

"The key to not getting ridiculously wasted is limiting yourself to only two drinks," Chase said, sipping his drink. "So pace yourself, so you don't run out quickly."

Following his advice, I put my glass down so I wouldn't be tempted to take another sip.

"How come Rebecca's so accepting of this? Technically, we're breaking the law," I remarked.

"Well, she has European beliefs. Like in Italy and France, they learn how to drink responsibly at a young age," Chase explained. "Rebecca feels that if we do the same now, in our late teens, we won't go overboard when we're 21."

Rebecca is the kind of person who's more logical than any other Congressman. My mother, on the other hand, doesn't dare question the lawmaker's decisions, because they must know better. But without a doubt, Rebecca is the one who knows better. Even if she was doing something "wrong" like breaking the law, she was still right.

"You know, you're really lucky to have Rebecca as your mother. She's the most amazing woman I've ever met, and I hope to be like her some day."

"I know. That's why I'm more worried about her than myself. If something happens to my dad, knock on wood; it's going to be harder on her. Of course, I'll be devastated, heart broken, and mournful, but I have it easier. In a year, I'll go off to college, be surrounded by people, start my own life. But if my dad dies, she'll be alone. She's a remarkable, wonderful person and she doesn't deserve that," Chase said, his voice trembling. His leaned forward, and hunched his shoulders together. "I feel like cancer is tearing my family apart. He can't die, it's too soon! He doesn't deserve this either! He's too kind, too considerate, and too great of a man. I look up to him the way that you look up to Rebecca. I can't lose him, and neither can my mother. And the worst part is I can't do anything about it to help or make it better, because it's out of my control."

Chase broke in sobs. It didn't sound anything like my sobs, let alone any other female's cry, because it was harsher and huskier. Resting on my knees, I draped my arms around his shoulders and pressed the side of my face into his back.

Before comforting him with my words, I used my gestures. Sometimes letting a person cry it all out first is better than trying to reassure them immediately.

When his sobs died off, I said, "You can help him, and you already decided that you will." Chase turned slightly, his face puzzled in confusion. "By seeing him. It's going to make him so happy, and that happiness will give him the strength to keep going, to keep fighting for something, someone. Just stand by his side, give him faith and courage, let him know that you love him, and he will get better, I promise. If you do that, he won't give up on you and Rebecca, he'll fight with every bit of strength left in him."

"I'm not ready to take over as man of the house," Chase said firmly, acknowledging my words of wisdom, but unable to reply to them.

"And he's not ready to resign," I replied.

Chase nuzzled his face into my shoulder. Taking his jaw line into my hands, I wiped his moist face.

"Let's not dwell on this. I don't want to ruin our awesome, fun filled night," he said, regaining himself. That's my boy, making a fast recovery.

"Of course not," I said, flashing him a reassuring smile. "Now tell me, what's included in this fun-filled night?"

Instead of answering me, Chase pulled out portable iHome speakers and his iPod. Cranking the volume, Wilson Pickett's song Land of 1000 Dances started blasting through the speakers. Chase started bopping his head in rhythm, catching a funky groove. Then, the music overwhelmed him and he jumped up and started dancing (it was more like kicking and thrusting) in the sand. Chase started belting the chorus, swinging his arms all around, jolting his legs in rapid beats, and even throwing in a few booty shakes. The sight of his frenetic dancing brought me to laughing hysterics.

"Come on!" He pulled me up to my feet. "NAH, NAH, NAH, NAH, NAH, NAH, NAH, NAH, NAH, NAH!"

He spun me around in circles, as my blood started flowing. I threw in the classic mash potato move my mother taught me when I was ten. The music was flowing through my veins, and my body reacted. Before I knew it, I was a dancing fool, just like Chase.

By this point it was dark, which meant nobody was around to see our humiliating dance moves. However, any of the neighbors who may have looked out their window, were in for a treat. A video camera should have captured this brilliant performance.

Out of breath, we collapsed onto the sand, laughing at ourselves.

"Aren't we full of energy today? First, jet skiing, now power dancing," I said, catching my breath.

"We'll recharge your battery, because you've got more to do," Chase said, bouncing back up. He started running, and called over his shoulder, "Follow me! I've got to show you something."

Chapter 26

After a long distance of running, Chase stopped us upon the rocks of the Jedi. Without fear, he effortlessly hopped from rock to rock. On the other hand, I struggled a bit more: High leveled boulders + my klutziness + darkness = falling to my death. As I traveled the Jedi path, I passed small groups of people, who were either standing in semi-circles or squatting on the cold boulders.

Once I caught up to him, Chase grabbed my wrists and pulled me close to him. Extending his finger, he pointed in the direction of dozens of ships lit up in neon colors.

"What is this . . .?" I whispered.

"You'll see," Chase replied, leaving me in anticipation. "Any minute now."

The wind and the drop in air temperature on the Jedi brought goose bumps to my skin. Crossing my arms around my chest, I leaned into Chase's silhouette, trying to absorb his body warmth. He tightened his grip around me, and rubbed my arms, trying to create heat friction.

Just as my teeth started chattering, I heard a BANG sound, followed by colorful designs illustrated in the sky.

"Fireworks," I commented, in delight. Smiling, I tilted my head to glance at Chase. "Why haven't I seen these before?"

"Because, this is the first firework show of the season," Chase replied. "It's kind of a tradition we have here, to put on a show to brighten up the communities spirits after an earthquake. It's put on by the locals, for the locals, so it's rather infamous."

"It's wonderful," I said, kissing his cheek. We watched in admiration, dazzled by the stunning chemical reactions. "So let me get this straight, you guys put on fireworks for earthquakes, but not for the fourth of July?"

"You should know by now that Santa Monica isn't exactly normal…"

Considering I had seen more drama, felt more pain, and experienced more surprises in my two months spent in Santa Monica than my 17 years spent in Connecticut, I couldn't help but agree.

When the show was over, we scurried back to our spot on the beach. Still cold, Chase ran inside and gathered a bundle of blankets for us to share. He made us a little bed, and snuggled up beside me. I laid my head on his chest as we looked up at the stars.

"Hey Chase?"

"Yeah?" Chase replied, running his fingers through my hair.

"What's going to happen to us when the summer is over?"

This question caused Chase to sit up and look at me. "I don't know ..."

"We're running out of time," I said, dropping my voice.

"I know. But I have no clue what's going to happen ..."

"Me either," I muttered, the topic starting to worry me. "Do you want to stay together?"

"Of course I do," Chase said, but his eyes narrowing. "But having a relationship with someone 3,000 miles away is difficult."

I raised my eyebrows and said, "What if I stayed here? What if I moved in with you guys and went to school here!"

Hopefully, I anticipated his reaction. But his face only dropped further.

"As great as that would be ... let's face it, that wouldn't blow over well. What about your friends, your family, your home in Connecticut. It's too much to ask for you to stay here and leave all of that behind."

"But I want to stay with you," I said, my voice shaking ever so slightly. "I'd give all of that up to be with you."

Chase took my face in his warm, calloused hands. "You say that now, but that's something you'll later regret."

"No ... I wouldn't!" I insisted, tears streaming down my face.

He wiped the tears away, then pulled me into a hug. "Let's not talk about this anymore, okay? Let's not talk about this until it's time." He pulled apart so he could look into my eyes. "We shouldn't dwell on the future, we should enjoy the present, enjoy the time we have left to be together."

Biting down on my bottom lip, I nodded slowly. Chase kissed me, then pulled me back down onto his chest.

"You see that?" Chase said, pointing at a constellation in the sky. "That's Andromeda. In the Greek myth, her mother, Cassiopeia, dared to say that she was more beautiful than the gods. To punish her for her blasphemy, Poseidon punished her by chaining her daughter to a rock as a sacrifice to a horrific sea monster. Perseus, the dragon slayer who also killed Medusa," Chase pointed to another set of stars, "saw Andromeda and fell in love with her. Perseus destroyed the monster by revealing the head of the Medusa, which would turn any living creature into stone. However, Andromeda's parents did not look away in time, and were also killed in the process. Poseidon took pity upon their souls, and casted them into the sky," Chase said, pointing to two constellations surrounded Andromeda's. "Thus, when both Andromeda and Perseus died, they too would also be placed in the heavens."

I wrapped my arms tighter around Chase's chest. His understanding of astronomy and mythology baffled me into affection.

"That's amazing," I whispered.

"Which part?"

"The story, and you're knowledge," I nuzzled my face into his chest. "Would you save me from an evil sea monster?"

"I would save you from anything," he said. "You should know that by now."

"When is it going to be my turn to save you? I've only taken care of you once . . ."

Chase pulled on my waist, so that I was laying on top of him. "Hayden, you already have saved me." I crinkled my eyebrows in utter confusion. "Look, I don't really like to talk about this, but you deserve to know. Before you came, I was going through a bit of a gloomy time. I wouldn't say I was depressed or anything, I was just in this weird, dark mood all of the time. I was always really quiet, I had a tough time dragging myself out of bed for school, I didn't hang out with many people, I closed myself off from everyone – I just always felt alone and empty inside. Jessica would have absolute fits, claiming I was too much to deal with and impossible to get through to."

I blinked my eyes in shock. "Why haven't I heard about this?"

"Like I said, I don't really bring it up too often. But when I heard you were coming, everything started getting better. Like the sunlight was starting to break through tiny slivers of the dark, grey clouds that surrounded my life. And then you arrived, and the sun broke through entirely, pushing away all the sad clouds. In a way, you did kind of save me. You brought me back to this fresh, cheerful state of mind. So, I owe you a thank you for that."

Again, I was shocked. But with the addition of speechlessness. This was something new, something unexpected, something I could have never predicted. I had contributed to his life in a way I never thought I could.

Instead of speaking, I kissed him. He rolled over, so that he was now on top. On the empty sandy beach, under warm and concealing blankets, we made love for the second time. Although it was less painful this time, it was just as powerful and magical.

We ended up sleeping there, outside on the beach, under the shimmering light of the stars. While it seemed like a good idea at the time, we both regretted it the next morning - with kinks and knots in our backs from uncomfortable sleeping and messy, greasy, tousled hair. My skin felt coated in a dry layer of sand.

"Babe, get up," I whispered, shaking a half-awake Chase.

With a moan, Chase forced himself to sit up. We were smart to put our clothes back on last night, because the populated beach was in seeing range. Both groggily, we took all of our supplies inside and took long, leisurely showers.

After the hot water washed away all of the sand, I twisted the knob to off. Tying my wet hair into messy bun, I got dressed into white jean shorts and a purple tank top.

Today was the day. Today, we would see John. Today, Chase would face his problems. Today, things would change.

In acclamation of the musical Rent, no day but today.

CHAPTER 27

Cold, grey, uncomfortable, foreign, haunting, lifeless.

Those words perfectly represented the aurora of John's treatment room. The walls were bland, empty, and suffocating to the human eye. There was one, small, bare window to the left of the room. An outdated television hung in the high corner of the room. A monitor, a white-sheeted hospital bed, and a few crummy chairs inhabited the rest of the room.

On the white, twin-sized bed laid John's shriveled up body. His complexion was pale and ghastly, matching the color of the walls. Dark circles bordered his sunken closed eyes, dry skin and wrinkles creased around his brows and lips. His remaining hair was grey, brittle, and untamed. Wires and machines were hooked up to his feeble face, hands, arms, and chest. Appearing to lose a dramatic amount of weight, he looked weak and fragile.

I looked up at Chase, whose face was twisting and contorting in pain of the horrendous sight. The only thing I could to do ease his pain was place a compassionate hand on his shoulder.

Rebecca and Chase, being immediate family, had first priority to greet him. Rebecca kissed his cold, wrinkled forehead, which caused John to open his tired, weary eyes. Chase sat down next to the bed.

"Hi Dad," Chase whispered, lightly squeezing his father's bony hand.

"Hey son." John's voice matched his appearance.

Just the sound of his father's battered and scratchy voice caused Chase to double over, sobbing into the edge of the bed. John slowly draped his fragile arm around his son's trembling shoulders. We all stood in silence as we watched the ultimate connecting moment; a son crying in the embrace of his sick father.

After a good, long cry, Chase sat up and rubbed his face.

"I'm fine," Chase muttered. Rebecca rustled his blond hair with her fingers. "I just need some water. I'll be right back."

After his departure, my family moved forward towards John, but still a few steps behind Rebecca.

"He looks good," John croaked.

"You can thank her for that," Rebecca turned and indicated to me. "I haven't seen him this lively in months."

John sent me a nod of gratitude. "Well I'm glad you've been able to pick up his spirits. After today, he's going to need you more than ever."

I crinkled my eyes in confusion. Why would today have a negative effect on Chase? It was supposed to help him. "I'm sorry, I don't understand."

My parents wandered to Rebecca's side, which left me standing alone.

"Honey, could you go get Chase?" Rebecca asked in a sweet yet forced tone, as if nothing was wrong. But I knew better. Something was definitely going on here, something strange.

Suspiciously, I did as she asked and searched the hallway for Chase. Fully recovered from his earlier break down, Chase was loitering near a vending machine, enthusiastically chatting away on the phone.

Strolling up behind him, I tried to pick up on as much as I could of his side of the conversation.

"Yeah . . . totally, that'd be chill . . . no I think it'd be really fun . . . yeah, I'll spread the word . . . yeah uh-huh . . . yeah I'll bring her . . . sounds good, see you later."

Unaware of my presence, Chase quickly turned around and bumped into me. I fell hard onto the cold, tiled floor.

"Oh, sorry Ace!" He apologized, pulling me back up to my feet. "I've got great news."

Ironic, I thought. He's got great news while his parents potentially had bad news.

"My friend, Nick, is throwing a 'going-away' party tonight because he's leaving for college next week. It sounds like fun, and I think we should really go. I think it'll be fun, actually going to a party as a couple, unlike last time. So what do you say, are you in?"

The real question was would he still want to go after our parents informed us on the most recent news. Of course, I had no idea what it was about, but something felt wrong. But, maybe I was just being pessimistic . . . depressing medical centers have that affect on me.

"Yeah, sure." My response was less than par on the energy, but it was the best I could do. "So our parents want to talk to us about something . . . I've been sent to fetch you."

"Both of our parents? Hmmm, a group parental decision," Chase pondered, walking beside me. "I wonder what it could be?"

And then he stopped dead in his tracks, his face expressing the sign of an epiphany.

"What if they've figured out some arrangement so we can stay together?!"

Wouldn't that be great, I bitterly thought. But something told me that definitely wasn't it. They wouldn't deliver such blissful news in such a depressing location.

Nevertheless, his optimism and hope was dumbfounding. "What put you in such a good mood? Was it the party?"

"No . . . I don't know, really. It felt really good to cry it out, because now I can look at the upside, you know? I'm seeing him for the first time, but it doesn't seem that bad. He seems to be getting a lot better, don't you think?"

I didn't really consider John's new deathly pale, shriveled up physique as indication of health improvements, but I tried to let Chase's cheerful attitude sway me.

When we entered, the room grew silent, and all eyes were on us. My mother and father looked concerned, Rebecca's smile looked pained, and John's eyes were red and watery. We were instructed to sit in the stiff, mismatching chairs.

"Chase . . . Hayden, this may be hard to swallow at first, but remember there's still hope, so don't give up on me yet. If you give up, I give up," John said. Although his voice was weak, he still had that strong vocal persuasion that caused us to obey him. "The cancer is now at stage four, which means it's starting to spread to my other organs. But they spotted it early, which means it's not over yet. I'm going to continue the Chemo, just in stronger dosage . . . the doctors say . . ."

His lips kept moving, but I couldn't hear what he was saying. The loud beat of my heart was thumping in my ears, overpowering all external sounds. I bent over, trying to ease the nausea that had formed in my stomach. My head started to spin and my vision blurred. Chase rubbed his hand up and down my back, trying to sooth me. I forced myself to look up at him and see how he was doing. His eyes were watery, but strong and determined, as he listened attentively to his father.

"Keep fighting Dad, I know you can do it." I heard Chase say, muffled by the tha-dump, tha-dump rhythm in my eardrums.

How was he so calm and collected? Why was I the nervous wreck? After all, it was his father, not mine! He just learned of the horrific severity of his father's life threatening illness! Just thinking about it made me feel even worse. I felt like was going to either pass out or puke. Putting my head between my thighs, I took steady deep breaths.

"We probably should take her home," I heard Rebecca say.

I listened as everyone said their goodbyes. I heard Chase say he would visit sometime later this week.

Chase helped me up, took my arm and wrapped it around his neck so that I could lean on him for strength. My legs felt feeble and weak, as if they would give out any minute.

"Bye Uncle John," I said, as I passed by the bed, no louder than a whisper. Remarkably, he heard me.

"Bye kiddo," he replied, his voice tender yet wretched.

My vision was blurry and out of focus, so Chase guided me down the halls, through the elevator, and into the back seat of the car. I curled up into a ball and rested my head on Chase's lap. He tenderly stroked my hair, as he gazed out of the car window.

Tragedy had struck John's life. Each day, the fight was getting harder. Each day, the cancer was growing stronger. Each day, the hopes were getting weaker. Each day, the possibilities were gaining weight. Each day, the statistics were gradually decreasing. Each day, the fear of death multiplies.

When we got home, Chase escorted me to my bed, and tucked me in. He placed a cold, wet cloth on my forehead.

"Why am I always the wreck?" I weakly asked him, disappointed in myself.

"Because you're you," Chase said. "And you have a big heart, an irrational mind set, and a clumsy physical coordination."

Scowling, I moaned in response. "I wish I didn't."

"I wouldn't want you any other way. I love you just the way you are," Chase said, dabbing my forehead. "We don't have to go to the party if you don't want to."

"I'll be better by then, I still want to go," I replied. "Do you think you're alright to go?"

"I'm fine," Chase quickly said. He was acting very weird, like none of this was affecting him.

"Are you sure? I mean, stage four is a pretty big deal," I said, trying to get him to open up to me.

"Yeah, but I'm not worried," Chase said, very sure of himself. "I know he'll make it."

I got a feeling that I shouldn't persuade the topic any further. I didn't want to push him over the edge.

"Maybe after a shower, I'll feel better," I said, groggily sitting up. "Then we can have dinner and head over to the party."

"Okay," Chase said, "I might as well get ready too."

My shower took me a little longer than usual. My whole body felt heavier, which meant I was slower with every action. By the time I was finished, my bathroom was as steamy as a sauna and my fingers were wrinkly.

I wasn't really in the mood to get dressed up, so I threw on some jean shorts, a white tank top, and Chase's blue zip up hoodie that I never felt like returning.

Rebecca cooked her famous lasagna, which filled the house with mouth-watering aromas.

"When was the last time you had this?" Rebecca asked me, right as I shoved a mouthful of noodles into my mouth.

Quickly chewing, I said, "I think it was Chase's sixth birthday."

"That's right! We had lasagna and ice cream cake," Rebecca commented.

"Best birthday meal, ever," Chase added.

The table conversation continued, briefly hitting topics, but we all made sure to avoid bringing up the hospital visit. Right now, it seemed to be a testy and sensitive topic for everyone, except for Chase...

After we finished eating and cleared out plates, Chase and I left for the party. It was a short drive, just around the corner and down the street. Like every other party, people were dancing to the blaring music or congregating in large clusters. This party was much larger than the last one, which meant even more unfamiliar faces. You'd think that after spending over two months in Santa Monica, I would know more people.

However, I spotted somebody I knew. Dean caught my eye, sending vicious chills down my spine. He was dancing with some blonde, pink tank top wearing girl, whose back was turn to me. Poor girl, she deserved a fair warning. Unfortunately, I could not provide that for her with Dean literally standing in my way. If I saw her without him, I would give her my words of caution.

"Bro! I'm so glad you could make it!" A shaggy haired brunette greeted Chase.

"Awesome party. Nick, this is Hayden," Chase said, introducing me to the host.

"What a lovely lady," Nick joked, kissing my hand. I looked up at Chase, who was clenching his jaw in envy. "Drinks are in the kitchen, help yourselves!"

"Thanks," Chase said, suffocating his jealousy. "See you around."

Chase and I squeezed our way through the crowds, searching for people we both knew. Luckily, we found Carmen and Tyler snuggling on the couch in the living room. Obviously out of place, Carmen's band members surrounded the cozy couple.

"Hey guys," Chase interrupted, pulling us into the small gathering. Tyler and Carmen got up and greeted us.

"I didn't think you'd make it," Tyler said, clasping hands with Chase. "How was visiting your old man?"

Chase's eyes transitioned from radiant to darkly serious. "Fine."

Carmen shot me a concerned glance, but the only thing I could do was shrug. For the first time in our relationship, I had no idea what was going on with Chase.

"You missed it today, bro. Paul totally flipped out at the new junior lifeguard," Tyler explained, attempting to warm up Chase's cold disposition. "It was seriously priceless."

"I bet," Chase replied, monotone. "Look, I'm going to go get a drink. Ace, you want something?"

"I don't know, you tell me," I replied. Chase was obviously a better controlled drinker than me, so I gave him control.

"How about a beer? And you can have one refill." I nodded my head, and he headed towards the kitchen.

"I thought he was over this bullshit," Tyler said bitterly, once Chase was out of hearing distance.

"He is . . . he's just been acting weird all day," I replied, defending him.

"That's for sure. He's like bi-polar, one day he's chill and the next day he's an ass."

"Hey, watch it," I said. "He's going through a rough time, okay?"

"Yeah, well doesn't have to take it out on me. You must be blind if you didn't see that," Tyler said.

"See what?"

"See that Chase is totally sweet to you, but lashes out at Tyler," Carmen added. "I saw it too."

Maybe I was blind. "Look I don't know what's really going on with him. Today, when we visited John, he broke out crying in the first ten minutes. After that, he was perfectly fine. Even when we found out that the cancer has started spreading. It's like all of a sudden, nothing affects him, like there is this wall or something, protecting him, making him invincible … I don't get it."

"Maybe he's just trying to be mentally strong for once," Tyler said, more insulting than helpful. I rolled my eyes at him.

"I know you're offended right now, but would it kill you to be a little considerate for your best friend?"

Tyler crossed his arms, and leaned back on the couch - typical pouty, angst body language. Carmen shrugged and disappeared into the kitchen, probably for another drink.

I plopped down onto the edge of the coffee table across from Tyler.

"Just cut him a break, okay?"

"Sometimes, it just gets really aggravating," Tyler admitted.

"Believe me, I know." His anger had caused a lot of drama between us, more than imaginable. But it didn't make me love him any less. If he could love me for my flaws, then I could love him for his. "Look, let's not talk about that anymore. How are things with Carmen?"

Tyler instantly transformed into a gossip girl. "Amazing. She's so talented and beautiful and kind and smart . . ."

"Whoa, whoa, save the gushing for somebody else."

"Sorry, I just really like her." His thin lips formed an embarrassed smile. "I feel like a changed guy. This sounds kind of weird, but thanks for rejecting me."

I looked him straight in the eye, and said, "No problem."

"And thanks for giving me that extra push to go out with her. It was the best decision of my life."

"Somebody's a bit sappy," I teased.

"Guilty."

Tyler stood up and pulled me into a thankful hug, harmless of course . . . except Chase didn't seem to think so. It was bold enough to make Chase crack inside, break down his wall, and finally release his day-filled emotions.

"You just don't know when to stop, do you?" Chase's sharp voice boomed from behind us.

"Chase it's not what you think . . ." I reasoned.

"What I think is once a player, always a player," Chase spat, staring at Tyler. "I think I need to reconsider who my best friend really is."

"Chase, stop!" I exclaimed.

"I knew it was too good. You never liked Carmen, so why would you start? She's you're rebound girl, because her best friend rejected you for me. You always want what you can't have."

"You don't know what you're saying, Chase! He does like her! He's crazy about her, he was just thanking me for setting them up together," I said, defending Tyler, who was quietly lingering behind me.

"Have I taught you nothing? Tyler is a liar! He chose Carmen, because dating her means he'll still have a connection to you!"

"He's not that bad, Chase, and you know it," I growled.

"Hayden, stop!" Tyler's clear voice pierced through the air. "Stop fighting everyone else's battle. We're big boys, we can defend ourselves. Learn to stop getting involved in other people's business. Nobody likes a busybody." I was taken aback, insulted by my own friend.

"You'll pay for that," Chase threatened. "Nobody talks to her like that and gets away with it!"

"Watch me!"

Unlike every other fight I had witness this summer, this one was different. For once, Chase wasn't pinpointed as the bad guy. More or less, this time Tyler and Chase were both angry bastards, ready to fight it out to the death.

Tyler and Chase both lunged towards each other at the same time. Tyler used his force to bash Chase up against the wall. Chase resisted and knocked Tyler down with his body.

This time, I wasn't going to be the one to break up the fight. Not after what Tyler said. Instead, I ran into the kitchen, screaming for somebody to help and stop them.

Nick rushed into the living room, and a sea of people followed to watch the action. Carmen and I met eyes, horrified at our boyfriends' behavior.

"What happened?" She whispered, as we both watched the scene.

"It was mutual. First, it was just Chase. But all of a sudden, Tyler exploded with rage and fought back," I mournfully replied. Nick was in the process of not breaking up the fight, but simply moving it outside. Some people followed, while some people, like Carmen and I, remained inside.

"Yeah, Tyler's been pretty testy all day," Carmen said. "I guess Chase just set him off."

"Should we go check on them?" I asked.

"No, let's give them time. Maybe if we let them fight it out for good, they'll be able to move past it once and for all."

Maybe Tyler was right. Maybe I was a busybody. After all, I just suggested to go check out them so we could get involved if we needed to. Not to mention, I always broke up their fights, which would explain Carmen's theory. But lingering around for them to solve it themselves made me anxious.

Suddenly, we heard a loud crash come from outside. A sound larger and louder than anything caused by two human bodies fighting. The loud noise was followed by people screaming, barging through the doors.

"Somebody! Call 911!" Jessica, wearing that same pink tank top, exclaimed. She was the girl Dean was with, which would explain why I hadn't seen her all night. But I didn't have time to worry about that, something much bigger was happening.

Carmen and I nervously rushed outside to see what the commotion was about. The party had moved farther down the street, where all the action was happening. Carmen and I followed the crowd to get a better look.

"No … no, it can't be. No!"

There, at the end of the street, two severely crashed cars laid in disarray. The driver of the hunter-green Range Rover decrepitly emerged, but the driver of the black Jeep did not.

Chapter 28

One glance, one minute, one missing face was all it took to for me to know that everything was going to change.

Tyler tottered away from his battered Range Rover. Carmen and I pushed through the crowd, desperate to get closer. I intercepted Carmen's attempt to embrace Tyler.

"What happened? Where is he? What the hell were you thinking?" I pushed against his chest in hysterics, forcing him to answer my questions.

"Easy, easy," Tyler said, staggering backwards and rubbing his neck. "Can't you just see I was just in a car crash?"

"No shit, Sherlock! Why? What the hell were you thinking? Where's Chase?"

"The fight wasn't doing much; we're too equal of opponents. So we decided to settle it once and for all with a street race. May the best racer win," Tyler said, disoriented.

"You idiots! You could have gotten killed," Carmen cried, finally able to wrap her arms around her boyfriend.

"Killed?" I dropped my tone, and asked for the last time, "Where is Chase?"

"He's still trapped in his car ..." Tyler admitted.

My heart sank into my stomach, my hands grew clammy, and my throat was dry despite the lump that had formed. Urgently, I pushed past Tyler and ran as fast as I could towards Chase's crushed car.

Jeeps are infamous for their dangerous frame, which essentially causes them to roll over in accidents. Chase's car was no exception. Flipped over, the black jeep Wrangler was destroyed, dented, and demolished. The front window was smashed to pieces, the front body was crushed, the left side was indented, the engine was steaming from under the mangled hood, and countless other mechanic destructions that I can't identify. Bottom line, the sight was terrifying and the odds were slim.

Tears rapidly left my eyes as I choked back a sob. From the CPR class I took at school, I knew that a person should never pull someone out from a vehicle without proper medical assistance. There was nothing I could do to help, until the ambulance arrived.

"Please, Chase." I croaked the words between sniffles. Knowing he was most likely unconscious didn't stop me from trying. "You can't leave me ... not yet. Rebecca needs you even more than I do. She depends on you to pull through for her, for John, for the sake of the family!"

Imagining Rebecca without John and Chase only brought the sobs harder. The two men of her life, inches away from death.

"Godammit Chase," I yelled, suddenly filled with rage. I didn't care anymore if he could hear me or not. "Why did you have to go and do this? Why can't you see the damage you do? Why don't you understand that you've been hurting everyone around you for the past month! Fucking shit!"

I stepped away, mouth open in horror, hands shaking in rage. Tyler and Carmen were smothering each other, feet away from me. A wash of envy and abhor washed over me. Sure, everything was going to be okay for them. But not for me, not for Chase.

My mind no longer controlled my body movements, my bitter hate took over.

"You!" I ripped Tyler out of Carmen's arms. "This is your fault! You just had to push him, didn't you?" I shoved him, with all my force. "Are you happy now? Are you happy that your best friend is lying unconscious in the seat of his destroyed car? Are you happy that you finally got your revenge? Are you happy that you won?"

"I didn't win anything," Tyler exclaimed, cowering from my assaults.

"You won the race, that's what you wanted. You came out alive, while he may not even live to see the day!" I pushed him harder, remembering his words: may the best racer win.

Tyler locked his hands around my wrists. "Stop it, Hayden! Goddamit, Chase is starting to rub off on you." That alone got me to stop. Narrowing my eyes, I relaxed my muscles. Tyler's voice was calm but stern. "My turn to ask questions. Do you really think that I wanted this? You think I'm happy about this? Do you think that lowly about me? Chase and I may be going through a rollercoaster of a rough patch, but I would never wish him this fate ..."

"Just let me go," I said, tugging out of his grip. "Wish or not, it's done."

Rubbing my chaffed wrists, I wiped my nose and headed back for Chase's ruined car. In the past, I wasn't always there for him, to support, love, and understand him. Today would be the start of a change.

"Hayden!" Tyler called after me. "Did you ever consider that maybe the street race was Chase's idea? That maybe he's the one to blame."

"No. Even if he did, it's still your fault for not trying to stop him. Going along with it is just as bad as suggesting it," I snapped, before turning my back on him.

At last, the ambulance arrived. One paramedic examined Tyler, making sure he was in a stable condition. The others rushed to Chase's side, equipment and vehicle ready.

With some high-tech metal appliance, the EMTs pried open the driver's door. Gripping my untamed hair, I watched as they pulled Chase's limp, bloody, wounded body out from the bounds of the car.

"Excuse me," said one paramedic, who had tapped me on the shoulder. After answering a series of questions for her, she asked, "Would you like to ride in the ambulance with him?"

Dabbing another tear, I dolefully nodded. Chase now rested on an orange plastic stretcher in the back of the ambulance. The EMT told me to sit in a specific spot on his right side, where I wouldn't get in the way.

Activating the screaming sirens, the vehicle rapidly accelerated. With trained speed, the paramedics connected Chase to an oxygen mask, hooked his arm up to an IV, and began bandaging his wounds and limbs. Looking away, I suffocated a sob that was arising. It killed me to see him so weak, so fragile, so helpless, and so afraid.

I fought against my usual paranoia. I wouldn't allow myself to think about the what if's. Inviting those thoughts in would only be detrimental. Instead, I suffocated those pestering questions, and burrowed them deep inside of me.

I was admiring the resuscitative equipment in the rear of the vehicle, when suddenly I felt something grab my leg.

After a mechanical beep, an paramedic reported, "We've got consciousness."

Whipping my head around, I saw Chase's hand on my thigh. His eyes were open slightly, showing only a sliver of his blue irises.

"Hayden …" he quietly whispered, through the oxygen mask.

"I'm here," I reassured him, holding his hand tightly. "Don't speak, just relax."

Chase let out the smallest smile before advertizing his gaze up to the ceiling. His body remained motionless and his eyes drowsily blinked ever so often. But he never let go; his hand, his fingers, his palm never left mine.

When we arrived at the hospital unit, I immediately jumped out of the ambulance so they could rush Chase into emergency surgery. Unfortunately, I was not permitted to stay with him any longer, so I lingered in the waiting room, tapping my foot, anticipating Rebecca and my parents' arrival.

"We rushed over as soon as we got the call," Rebecca exclaimed, bursting into the scene. Her usual sleek blonde hair was tied into a messy bun, and her eyeliner was running beneath the crease of her eyelids. Obviously, two hospital visits for two separate men in one day was doing a number on her appearance. "Where is he? What's going on?"

"He's in surgery right now," I muttered.

"Oh God," she whimpered, collapsing onto a chair and burying her face in her manicured hands. "My two boys …"

"Rebecca, don't worry, they're both going to be okay," my mother cooed, trying to comfort her best friend in despair.

"I guess these Levine boys really dig the hospital today," my father said, trying to lighten the mood.

My mother glared at him and said, "Not helping."

"What am I going to do? I can't lose even handle losing one, what happens if I lose both?" Never in my life have I ever seen Rebecca so distraught. In a way, she was suffering more than they were. Her emotional and psychological pain was worst than Chase's and John's physical pain combined.

After a nail-biting wait, a nurse came out. "Your son is out of surgery and is now being moved to the Intensive Care Unit. You may see him now."

Chapter 29

The halls were bland, empty, and quiet, with just a few nurses wandering around. A wave of chills traveled through my body. I didn't know whether they were caused by the air conditioning, which was on full blast, or the anticipation of what awaited me.

The nurse led us to room 203, then left us to continue on our own. An attractive, middle-aged doctor loitered in front of the door.

"Hey everyone," he said, extending his hand out for a round of hand-shakes. "You must be the family. I'm Dr. Miller."

"Nice to meet you," Rebecca replied. "How's everything?"

"Not good, but not bad either," Dr. Miller reported, flipping through the pages on his clipboard. "Your son has acquired a great deal of damage to his body. He tore the ACL in his right knee, so we performed an Arthroscopic surgery. His left elbow and wrist are fractured, a few of his ribs are broken, and his deep gashes have been stitched up. Lastly, he's got a mild concussion and some internal bleeding."

As he listing all of the injuries, I couldn't imagine the kind of unbearable pain and suffering Chase was going through. My heart shattered into pieces as I thought of the agony he was experiencing.

"Oh God, it all sounds horribly dreadful," Rebecca muttered, her eyes filling with tears.

"I know it sounds like a lot, but look at the bright side. With a bit of time and physical therapy, he'll be able to make a full recovery," Dr. Miller pointed out, trying to lighten our spirits.

Hearing good news is always pleasing, but it never erases or numbs the present stage of tragedy. Eventually, Chase would get better, but right now, he was suffering.

At last, the wait was over. Dr. Miller turned the door handle, and allowed us inside. If I could put the emotional pain I felt into words, I would. But no word, no phrase, no expression can convey it. I snuck a glance at Rebecca and my mother, who were both crying like me. My father, standing strong, let one single tear fall from the corner of his eye.

Chase laid helplessly on the bed. A monitor and an IV were hooked up to his mangled body. The leg that had been performed on was wrapped and elevated in the air. His elbow, resting in a sling, was plastered up to his mid arm. Random patches of his skin were stitched up and wrapped in medical cloth. Bruises and open cuts were scattered around his body.

Rebecca scrambled to his side, kneeled down onto the cold floor, and held her son's good hand.

"My baby . . ." was all she managed to say before breaking into sobs. She bent over, smothering her face into Chase's mattress. Chase lifted his tan, good arm and rested it around his mother's shaking shoulders.

"It's going to be alright . . . I'm going to be fine, you'll see" he whispered, as he stroked the back of her head.

My father put his arm around me, and pulled me closer to him and my mother. Our family was distant, but unlike the Levines, we weren't being pulled apart by devastation. Watching their family fall to pieces was a wake up call. Our family had to learn to appreciate each other, appreciate what we had, before it was too late.

After her sobs faded, Rebecca sat up, took a deep breath, and wiped her eye make up.

"I'm okay . . ." with another deep breath, she continued. "I should probably go visit your father and fill him in."

Chase gave her hand one last squeeze before she got up.

"We should probably go with you," my mother suggested. "Is that okay with you, Hayden?"

"Yeah, no problem," I replied, thankful for some alone time with Chase.

I waited until they left to take a few, slow steps towards him.

"So … how do you feel?" I ran my hand over the white, metal bar of the bed's footboard.

"Like a peach," Chase said, sarcastically. I didn't know how to react to his comment; whether to laugh or smirk or even roll my eyes. Why was this so awkward and uncomfortable?

"Good," I finally said, as I sat down in leather chair by his bed.

"Why are you acting so weird?" Chase asked. "What's bothering you?"

"I don't know. Maybe because this is the worst possible way to spend our last two weeks together," I said, the tears rolling out of my eyes. My legs itched with exasperation, forcing me to stand up and pace around.

"I really screwed up, didn't I?" Chase sounded so regretful and ashamed of his actions. With his right hand, he grabbed onto mine. "Please, sit down, you're making me nervous."

"I can't," I said, through a quivering voice.

"Please Ace," Chase plead, his voice filled with desperation. "Come lay with me."

"I can't," I said, repeating myself.

"Stop saying that," Chase spat, obviously annoyed by my constant defiance. I finally forced myself to look at him directly in the eyes. His blue eyes were filled with discomfort and sorrow.

"I don't want to hurt you," I muttered.

"You won't," Chase reassured, looking deeply into my eyes.

His hand guided me to the left side of his body, so I wouldn't invaded his severely injured, freshly-operated leg. Taking up the free space on the left side of the bed, I curled up next to him. Due to his casted left arm, he wasn't able to embrace me. Instead, he stretched his right arm over his torso, so he could still hold my hand.

"Are you sure I'm not putting you at any discomfort?" I asked, looking down and tracing the outline of his calloused fingers.

"This is the most comfortable I've been all day," he replied. "Do you want to talk about everything?"

I took a pause, recollected my thoughts, and then answered honestly. "No."

"You won't even give me a chance to explain?"

"You don't need to, I already know it all," I said, my voice piercing through the cold air.

"That's the thing, you don't," Chase spat.

"Yes, I do. I've known you for seventeen years, I know you like the back of my hand. After your breakdown, you decided you never wanted to feel like that again, so you pushed it down and bottled up all of your emotions. You let them build up in side of you, but you couldn't hold them in for long, oh no," my voice shook, as I let go of his hand. "One jab from Tyler sent you over the edge. You cracked, releasing all of your emotions. You weren't thinking clearly, because you were so full of anger. So you suggested the idea of a street race, to finally prove yourself. Of course, due to your lack of mental sensibility, the crash happened and here we are now."

"I don't know if I should love or hate you for that," Chase muttered.

That's when I knew I nailed it, spot on. Overwhelmed, I stood up.

"You know what Chase? Sometimes I feel like this whole thing was a mistake. That we shouldn't have gotten together, that I shouldn't have come for the summer. Because sometimes I feel like the high points of our relationship don't make up for the low points. I feel like for every good moment, there's two bad ones. Sometimes, I feel like you're still the same little boy I used to know, and sometimes I feel like you're a complete stranger. And as much as I love you, which I always have and always will, sometimes I feel like it's not worth it."

"Ace, what are you saying?"

"I'm saying. . . ." I pondered, trying to detect the path I was taking. "I'm saying that maybe we should just forget this ever happened. Maybe, I should leave and go back to Connecticut, before we drag this out any further. To do so would only hurt us more."

"Hayden," Chase whispered. "You can't mean that, you aren't thinking clearly. I need you."

"What you need is some real emotional therapy, someone who can really help you," I said, letting the tears run down my face. "I wish I could help you, because you need it. But this is out of my hands. For months, I've been trying to help you, but there comes a time when enough is enough."

"Hayden, don't do this. What if I got help, what if I got better?"

"In two weeks? Even if you did, it wouldn't matter because the summer would be over anyway," I swallowed hard, "Don't do it for me, do it for yourself. I'm sorry, Chase."

I took one last look at him, scanning the features of his face, only guessing how long it would be until I saw him again. Another ten years? Another twenty? At last, I tore my eyes away from him. As much as it killed me to put him through so much pain (as if he didn't already have enough for one day) I knew it was for the better.

"Goodbye Ace," he whispered, as I ran out of the room, bursting into tears.

Why was I crying? There really was no point. I wasn't the one being dumped, I wasn't the one being left, I wasn't the one being given up on. This had been my choice, my decision. And as hard as it was, it was right thing to do.

And so, I left. I left without telling my parents, without explaining myself, without saying my goodbyes. I knew it was disrespectful and I knew it would earn myself a life time of grounding, but I didn't care. All I cared about was leaving – leaving this hospital, leaving this town, leaving this state, leaving everything that was associated with this summer.

I told the taxi driver to wait fifteen minutes, while I gathered my belongings. When my bags were packed, I took one last look around the house. When I first arrived, everything was so beautiful, so new, so foreign. Now, two months later, this was my second home. But just like their old home in Connecticut, it would be replaced by something else in my life and become a figment of my memories … just like everything else.

I left a note on the kitchen counter, telling my parents where I was going. I left a second note for Rebecca, expressing my apologies, my love, my gratefulness, and my prayers.

And with that, I left. Closing the front door to the Levine's beach house, I closed another chapter of my life.

CHAPTER 30

4 MONTHS LATER

Life back in Connecticut dragged on slowly. Everything felt different, even though nothing had really changed.

Running out, disobeying my parents, and using their credit card number to pay for my plane ticket back home earned me two months of grounding. And despite all the nights I spent at home, laying around, staring at the ceiling, not once did they bring up California. They knew better than to.

Sometimes at night, I could hear my mother's voice through my bedroom wall when she was talking to Rebecca on the phone. Most times, I tuned out my mother's side of the conversation, knowing it was better to just block that part of my life out. But on rare occasion, I would indulge and take a listen, waiting for my mother to say, "I'm glad to hear everything's going well."

Everyday was a blur. In the morning, I could barely get out of bed. During the school day, I couldn't focus. When I got home, I locked myself in my room, laid on my bed, and stared out the window.

A few weeks after school started, my parents addressed their concerns about me. When they brought it up, they deliberately avoided any reference to the summer. Instead, they attacked my recently adapted attitude. When they recommended I see a shrink, I got up, walked up the stairs, and slammed my bedroom door. I couldn't blame them for that – they didn't know that the reason I broke up with him was because he needed therapy – but still the wound had been opened, and the pain was uncontrollably pouring out of me.

Since that day, I always questioned if I was the one that truly needed the psychological help. Was it normal to let a break up affect me this much? Was I emotionally stable? Maybe I was a hypocrite. Maybe I should have taken a look in the mirror before making the biggest mistake of my life.

But the damage had been done, and I had to live with the consequences.

As for my friends, they tried their best to understand. They tried their best to be sympathetic towards me, even though they didn't know why to be. They tried to their best to accept my new behavior, although they didn't know what had caused me to change.

As the days, weeks, months went on, the pain started to numb. The hot, burning pain that I felt turned into icy, cold emptiness.

One, chilly, December day after school, the unexpected happened.

After the last period bell rang, I slugged on my backpack, buttoned up my coat, and walked out the school's front doors. The sky was darkly grey, emitting an ugly haze around the environment. But through the fog, I saw him.

He stood there on the other side of the road, perfectly healthy, leaning against the side of his newly refurbished black jeep that was parked on the curb. His blonde hair was darker and shorter, his tan had faded, and his summer beach clothes were replaced by winter attire.

Every emotion inside of me flipped, causing a mental cat-astrophe. I was covered in sweat and in goose-bumps. I was filled with pain and pleasure, anger and happiness, sadness and gladness.

What should I do? What should I say? How should I possibly feel?

My body felt like it was being torn into a million pieces, as my world came crashing down.

Finally, I got my locked, brittle legs to move me forward. I approached him ever so slightly, keeping my distance. My limbs tensed up as I forced myself to stay calm.

"Hayden . . ." he said, with relief in his voice. When he said my name, it felt so foreign, that I didn't even respond to it. My mind didn't recognize my name when he said it. He stared at me for a moment, just waiting. But I couldn't do anything, I couldn't respond how he wanted me to. Eventually, he said, "You look good."

My cheeks burned with fury. How could he say that to me? That I look good after he made my life a living hell? Suddenly, I was reminded of the cruel reality – he didn't do this to me, I did this to myself.

"You too," I croaked, hit with the world's weight.

He moved forward, wrapping his arms around my motionless body. I didn't stop him. I let his warmth fill me up, to the point where I closed my eyes and forgot about everything. I let his hug bring me back to the first hug we shared seven months ago, back when I first arrived at the airport. I was reminded of how good it felt to be back in his arms. My arms gently wrapped around his broad waist.

"Losing you . . . was the best and worst thing that has ever happened to me," he whispered, before pressing his soft lips into mine.

That kiss was all I needed to be reminded of what we shared. Love was something powerful, something that could overcome any distance, any struggle, any problem, and any obstacle. To deny love when found was a crime in itself.

When we broke apart, I noticed that the sun's light had beaten through the dark, gloomy sky.

Epilogue

If there's one thing that I have learned in the past few years, it is that everything happens for a reason. Sometimes, I felt powerless and I had to wonder "why do these things happen to me?" but I realized that crying over the past won't change it and worrying about the future wouldn't make it turn out perfectly. There's only one way to live life with total certainty, and that is to take it day by day. You can't drive looking out of the rearview mirror, you have to keep moving forward. You never know which day could be your last.

A month before the end of my senior year, I received news that John, the man who loved me as much as my own father, had passed away. I originally didn't want to go back to California for his funeral, I didn't want to have to see Chase. After his unannounced visit to Connecticut, our relationship was left unclear.

"I love you too much to mess up again," he said when I dropped him off at the airport.

I spent months pondering what exactly he meant by that, afraid to ask for fear of total rejection. I finally retired the incessant worry after I decided my goal should be to finish high school, not to fix my relationship with Chase. I pushed my selfishness aside, and packed my bag. I owed it to John.

At the funeral, I was a mess. Between my bouts of hysteria, I saw Chase out of the corner of my eye. He was seated by his mother, holding her hand while she cried. He wore the expression of a worn man, someone who had been through far too much. When he saw me looking, I gave him a weak, sad smile. Handsome as ever, he nodded lamentably in response as a single tear rolled down his cheek.

When I returned home, I finished out my last month of high school. I graduated and then spent the entire summer working full-time to distract myself from being flooded with memories of the previous summer.

When fall arrived, I was enrolled at the University of California, Los Angeles. It was a tough decision, but I knew that I wanted to live in California from the day I arrived for the first time, just over a year before. When things with Chase went sour, I dropped my dreams of college there completely. I couldn't bear the idea of living so close to the place where my life changed forever. After some soul searching, I knew I couldn't let a boy stop me from living my dreams.

By spring I had a boyfriend, and after I got over my trust issues, I moved in with him by the following fall. Now, I was in my second year of college, working on a major in early childhood education and my life seemed to be falling into place.

"Good morning," a deep, husky voice said behind me. "Have you seen my Economics textbook anywhere?"

"Check the living room," I said, smiling. His blonde hair was messy from just waking up, giving him a hot, disheveled look. I felt my heart leap as he turned around. I couldn't believe this boy was mine. He was so... perfect. "I'll get started on breakfast, okay?" I turned around and started searching the refrigerator for eggs.

"Oh, Hayden," he said. "I wanted to ask you something else."

"Sure," I replied, without even turning around. "Go for it." I felt a tap on my back so I spun around quickly. When I saw him on one knee I immediately burst into happy tears.

"Hayden, I know I am not perfect, and I have messed up more times than I can count, but I promise I will love you everyday for the rest of my life, if you'll have me. Will you marry me?"

I looked at the elegant ring in the box, and then met his beautiful, blue eyes. "Of course!" I exclaimed. I was smiling like a huge dork as he slipped the ring on my finger. I helped him up off of the kitchen floor before pulling him into an embrace.

"I love you," he whispered into my ear.

"I love you more, Chase." I replied.

"That's impossible," He laughed. "Nobody could ever love anyone more than I love you." He pulled my face toward his and kissed me passionately.

We were the success story; the childhood lovers who had once gone their separate ways, only to have their paths cross once again.